Bellualis Chron

C000136302

Golem

E J Parry

HEDDON PUBLISHING

First edition published in 2019 by Heddon Publishing

ISBN 978-1-913166-09-0

Cover design by Catherine Clarke
Images courtesy of
© AdobeStock #197520368
© AdobeStock #109551417
© AdobeStock #70828618

Book design and layout by Heddon Publishing.

www.heddonpublishing.com
www.facebook.com/heddonpublishing
@PublishHeddon

for Mona, Ethan and Neve

1.

"**D**o it," he said. "Go on, do it. It'll be a laugh."

The boy took a deep breath to steady his nerves and waited for the right moment to move. He was hidden in an old mop cupboard, deep in the shadows, left on his own. The other two, his 'mates', as he sarcastically thought to himself, had left him there. One of them had bottled it, calling the whole thing a bad idea and backing out, whilst the other one – the one whose idea this was – had mocked him when he had questioned it; called him a chicken for not being sure, and had kept daring him over and over again to do it, before clearing off as well. Those threatening words, the name-calling and jeering, were still ringing round in his head, taunting him.

"This will be epic," he had said. "The best prank of them all. But if you're too chicken to do it…? If you're too scared? If you're a coward and too frightened, then maybe you should back out, too?" The boy had laughed at him, calling him more names and taunting him before running off, leaving him on his own. Of course, the others had warned him it was a bad idea and that he shouldn't listen to those boys, but he couldn't back off. Who could?

Anyway, he thought, *I'll show them. I'm no bottler. I won't back down from any dare. I'll do it and then I'll dare them to do something even bigger and we'll see who's scared then!*

He held the lighter in one hand, crouching down; hidden from view. He flicked at it nervously as he waited. One by one, the teachers eventually left the staffroom, moving off to their lessons, but he wouldn't be joining them. He wouldn't be in class that afternoon. He was going to show all of his mates that he wasn't chicken.

The dare was a dangerous one; a step up from the ones they usually did. To get into the staffroom and set fire to the bin. No one would be hurt and the fire wouldn't spread. It would just fill the room with smoke, which would be hilarious, but now that he was here, alone, it didn't seem so funny. He was scared and nearly managed to talk himself out of it but a dare was a dare and he didn't want to imagine how bad the name-calling and mickey-taking would be if he didn't do it.

When he was convinced that all of the teachers had gone, he quietly crept out of his hiding place and went over to the staffroom door. He put his ear against it and listened for any sounds coming from within the room. All was silent so he made his move. Carefully and quietly, he opened the door, ready to make a run for it at the slightest hint of anyone coming near, or returning.

He crept into the staffroom and pulled the door closed behind him. Immediately, he was hit by a horrific stench, which made him want to vomit. It was like fetid rotting flesh, mixed with bad breath and stale body odour. He shook his head vigorously, trying to ignore the smell, and reminded himself of what he was there to do. He needed to be quick: get in, do the job, and then get out. Breathing through his mouth, he scanned the room, looking for the bin. He spotted it in the far corner. *I'll show them who's scared*, he thought, bending down and pulling a piece of paper from it. He held it out in front of his face, lit it and watched as the flames started to build and grow higher. He was just about to put it back in the bin to complete the dare when he heard a noise. *Clack, clack, clack.* He froze, terrified by the familiar sound, then felt something grab him from behind, around his neck.

He dropped the burning paper to the floor as he was lifted clean off his feet and into the air. A black-heeled boot deliberately stood on the flames, extinguishing them.

He tried to shout but he couldn't. Kicking and struggling, he grabbed at the strong hand that was slowly choking him, but he couldn't free himself. The iron-like grip tightened around his neck as he was turned around to face his captor. He looked into her dark eyes as she pressed a cold, sharp finger against his forehead. Immediately, he felt all of his resistance leave him and he hung there, helpless in her grip, looking into her sneering face.

The room turned white and everything but her seemed to disappear. As his eyes closed, he heard her speak.

"Naughty little boys must be punished."

2.

Sophie Clearwater stood in front of the large gates of Thornberry Woods High School and took a long, deep breath. On either side of the gates stood an intimidating large red-brick wall, which seemed to go on forever and surrounded the school grounds on all sides. *Keeping everything safely within,* she thought with a little shiver.

Sophie wasn't the tallest of girls. She had dark, hazelnut-coloured eyes and long mousey-brown hair, which she normally wore in a ponytail. She felt uncomfortable looking at Thornberry Woods and thought about her old school, and all of the friends that she had left behind. It was late January, the school year was well under way, and she hadn't wanted to leave at all, but she understood why her family had to move.

She had been dragged down here, to the middle of nowhere, just after her fourteenth birthday, when her dad's job had changed. This was to be a new start for them all. The dark grey clouds shifted ominously overhead, adding a sense of menace and foreboding to her already troubled thoughts. However, it was the first day of her new life at her new school, and she was determined to make it work. She slowly let out her breath and walked through the gates.

Thornberry Woods was ancient. The building had been in the village for as long as anyone could remember. Sophie pulled her coat close against the wind and tried to shrink inside it as she slowly walked down the long driveway, which was flanked either side by huge towering oak trees that had been there for as long as the old building had. The only sounds were the cold wind blowing as the leaves whipped around her feet, and her own heartbeat, pounding inside her head. At the end of the drive stood an old stone archway. She approached it slowly and shivered as she looked at her new school.

The building seemed to reach up to the sky. In another life, it had been a stately home, and then a convent. Its role now, however, was as a secondary high school, part of the 'Triumphi in Robore' Academy. It had old stone turrets and ugly gargoyles across its roof. They looked as though they were keeping watch on all those who entered.

Sophie looked across the school yard. She was used to seeing children running around; shouting and chasing each other whilst they waited to be let in. She was used to balls flying through the air and the sights and sounds of fun and laughter. This yard was very different. The first thing she noticed was how quiet everything seemed. No one seemed to be laughing or playing; instead, there was just a low murmuring of whispers and quiet conversation.

The wind continued to blow cold and hard as Sophie walked towards the school entrance. Not one child looked at her, or even seemed to notice her. They were all too engrossed in their own hushed conversations or quiet activities. She approached a small group of children who were huddled together, sheltering from the cold wind. Sophie smiled nervously, hoping they would smile back and make her first morning slightly more bearable. They ignored her and seemed to huddle even closer together, quietly whispering to each other. Sophie suddenly felt very vulnerable, standing alone in the school yard. It was as though she could feel a hundred eyes all watching and studying her, waiting to see what she would do next. She hurried through the two large oak doors that gave entrance to the building, out of the cold wind and her imagined vulnerability, and into the school, making her way to the reception, where she was greeted by the sight of an incredibly large woman sitting at a computer. The woman looked like a huge slug, sitting on a chair that was far too small for her overly large frame.

"Good morning." Sophie smiled nervously at the large receptionist. The grotesque, slug-like woman didn't respond or even look up from her screen, leaving Sophie to stand awkwardly waiting.

After an uncomfortably long silence, Sophie tried again, her voice shaking slightly. "Good morning."

"Wait," rasped the woman. Her eyes bulged widely as she typed a few more words before finally looking up at Sophie. She licked her lips and smiled. Her teeth were brown and rotten and her smile made Sophie shudder.

"Good morning. I'm Sophie May Clearwater," the young girl announced. "I'm new here and I'm not sure where to go." The old slug began typing on her keyboard, her yellow eyes never leaving Sophie. After what seemed an eternity, she looked back down at her screen.

"Year 9, Mrs French's classsss," she rasped without looking back at Sophie. "Peter here will show you the way." A young boy Sophie hadn't noticed appeared next to the slug woman. He had a small orange badge pinned to his blazer lapel.

"Yes Miss Thomass." He replied, nodding courteously. He looked at Sophie and gestured to her to follow him. As she walked along the corridor, away from the office, Sophie could feel the yellow-tinged eyes of Miss Thomass fixed on her, watching until she was out of sight.

"What's it like here?" Sophie asked Peter, who was staring straight ahead as if he didn't know she was there.

"Thornberry Woods is an outstanding school," he replied, eyes still fixed straight ahead. "Ms Malignus has turned this school around and created a marvellous learning environment. We are privileged to be here." He turned to Sophie as if noticing her for the first time. "Please walk along the left side of the corridor in single-file. Talking is not permitted in the corridors," he instructed before continuing the journey.

He's a bit odd, she thought to herself, falling in behind him, but she remained quiet as they walked through the school. It was warm and still and the corridors were long and wide, lined with equally-spaced closed classroom doors. Apart from the occasional bookcase or cabinet, there was no furniture to be seen, which gave the school a cold, sterile feeling; a legacy from its days as a convent.

"Here is Mrs French's class," Peter eventually announced after they had turned into the appropriate bland corridor. He opened the door and escorted Sophie into the empty classroom before leaving her and making his way elsewhere.

Sophie looked around the room. The walls were painted cream. Each display was backed with a blue border and was perfectly in line with the one next to it. The tables only had space for two children to sit at and were positioned in neat rows, all facing forward. It was a functional room, with no plants or anything else that might be a distraction.

It could be worse, Sophie thought, as she went to the window and looked out at the grey skies and the yard below, where the children lined up neatly, ready to be brought in, leaves whipping around them in the wind.

She sat at a desk and waited for her new teacher and new class to arrive.

3.

Mrs French entered the room first. She was a short, stumpy woman, with a large double chin. She reminded Sophie of a fat, squat toad. She looked at Sophie, who had remained sitting in her seat, and somehow narrowed her bulbous eyes. "It is customary in this school to stand when a teacher enters the room mmm, mmm," she croaked.

"Sorry, Miss," Sophie stuttered, immediately standing up.

"What have we here mmm, mmm?" wheezed Mrs French, waddling toward the girl and licking her lips with a big fat tongue. Sophie was surprised to find that she was a bit taller than her teacher.

Mrs French leaned in uncomfortably close to Sophie and peered at her over thin-wired glasses, looking her up and down. Sophie strongly felt as though she was being inspected.

"Mmm, mmm," the teacher muttered to herself. She leaned in so close that Sophie could smell her foul breath. A stale, musty smell was also coming from the woman. She licked her lips and smiled, showing a row of sharp, pointy little teeth. Sophie discreetly tried to lean away from the old toad. "Mmm, mmm… will do, will do," Mrs French muttered to herself, finally waddling away from the girl.

Sophie quickly sat back down in her chair, feeling slightly uncomfortable due to the strange behaviour of her teacher. Mrs French disappeared into the stock cupboard, leaving the girl to sit alone in the classroom once more. Sophie felt as though she had been sitting and waiting for an eternity by the time the rest of her class began to arrive from the outside yard. She felt a wave of relief flush over her. *Thank goodness*, she thought as she looked at her new classmates. She smiled at one or two, trying to appear friendly, but she didn't get a response from any of them as they entered the room one by one, in complete silence. The uncomfortable feeling in Sophie's stomach began to grow. None of the children sat down. Instead, they all stood silently behind their desks and stared forwards, waiting.

Sophie was the only person in the room who was seated so she slowly stood up, not wanting to be the odd one out, and stood silently like the rest of her classmates, waiting for their teacher.

Mrs French emerged from her stock cupboard. She looked at her class and licked her lips. "Mmm, mmm." She studied them all, eyes wide and glinting excitedly. "Good morning, children."

"Good morning, Mrs French," the children answered with a robotic, monotonous tone.

"You may be seated." Quietly, the children sat down and waited. "I trust you all had a fun-filled weekend mmm, mmm?" The teacher licked her lips slowly.

No one responded.

"Good, good. Before we do anything else," she announced to the class, looking directly at Sophie, her eyes bulging wide, "I'd like us to welcome a new student who is joining us today. This is Sophie May Clearwater, mmm, mmm."

She beckoned Sophie to the front of the room. At first, Sophie shook her head, mortified at being asked to the front of the class. She thought she would die of embarrassment but Mrs French was quite insistent that she should do as she was being instructed. Reluctantly, Sophie walked to the front, where the teacher stood. Mrs French put her hands on Sophie's shoulders and gently squeezed her. A flash of greedy excitement quickly appeared in the teacher's wide eyes. It just as quickly disappeared. She spun Sophie around to face the class. "Say hello, class."

As one, the class responded in that same monotonous drone: "Hello, Sophie."

"Good, good," continued Mrs French. "Mmm, mmm." The class sat silently waiting as Sophie quickly returned to her desk. She was next to another young girl, who was staring forward.

"Penelope," Mrs French called, "you can look after Sophie. Ensure she knows the school rules. It is important that we abide by them at all times, Sophie. Also, Penelope, make sure that she is given a timetable and goes to the correct classes mmm, mmm."

"Yes, Mrs French."

Sophie smiled at Penelope. She was a tall girl with long, plaited hair and an orange badge pinned onto her uniform. Penelope stared forward into the distance and didn't even turn to look at her. Sophie could feel herself sinking further into her seat.

"James," Mrs French called to a boy with neatly combed hair, who was seated at the front of the room. He was staring ahead and didn't turn to look at Mrs French as she spoke to him. "Please line up and lead the class to the hall for assembly mmm, mmm."

"Yes, Mrs French."

James stood up and moved to the door. He too was wearing an orange badge, like Penelope's. One by one, in the order of how they were seated, each child stood up and quietly joined James in the line. Sophie quickly copied and stood next to Penelope. Once the queue was complete, Mrs French gave a signal for James to lead the way through to the hall. The teacher followed at the end of the line.

As they walked, Sophie couldn't help but notice other lines of children, all walking along the left side of the corridor, heading towards the old school hall. Each was followed by a teacher and all were eerily silent.

When they arrived in the hall, the children sat down in tight rows. Mrs French joined the other teachers sitting at the front of the hall on a small, slightly raised stage and quietly spoke with them. Sophie thought they looked an odd mix of people. Some were fat and stumpy; others were long and stick-like; one teacher was covered with hair, whilst another was completely bald. All of them looked peculiar in one way or another and were unlike any teachers she had seen before. She looked around the hall at the faces of her new school mates. They were all facing forward and silently looking towards the front of the room, where the teachers sat.

Apart from the muted whispers of the teachers, not a sound could be heard in this eerily silent place. Sophie noticed that some of the children had blank, detached looks on their faces, whilst others looked almost frightened to be there. She caught the eye of a girl with short black hair, who looked about the same age as her and was sitting a few rows away. They looked at each other for a fraction of a second before the girl quickly looked away, distracted by a sound which was growing in the distance and was slowly breaking the silence that had built.

Clack, clack, clack went Ms Malignus's boots, gradually getting louder as she entered the hall.

4.

Ms Malignus marched purposefully into the hall. Sophie recognised her instantly as the head of the school. She had met her previously when she had first visited with her parents and the woman had reminded Sophie then of a large, incredibly skinny stick insect, with long, spindly limbs and sharp, bony features. She had black hair, which she had in a tight bun at the top of her head, and glasses that perched upon the end of her long nose. Sophie's parents had laughed at their daughter's description of the Head and reminded her of the school's outstanding reputation. Sophie hadn't liked the look of Malignus at their first meeting and hadn't changed her opinion of her now.

As she made her way through the rows of children, Ms Malignus glared at them, full of hate and disgust, and seemed to study those she passed. Most of the children kept their heads down and looked at the floor, avoiding any chance of making eye contact with her, whilst others continued to stare forwards. Sophie noticed that the teachers on the small stage were starting to fidget and seemed to be growing excited as she drew nearer to them. Mrs French had a huge smile on her face and her large eyes were almost popping out of her head. A teacher in a blue shirt sat rubbing his hands. He was grinning broadly, his eyes fixed on the Head as she made her way through the hall. He had large sweat stains clearly showing through his shirt and which appeared to be spreading as she approached him. One fierce-looking teacher didn't seem to be looking at Ms Malignus but appeared to be scanning the room, glancing quickly at the children, his eyes quickly moving back and forth like some big insect searching for something. The silence in the room was deafening, punctuated only by the *clack, clack, clack* of the Head's black heeled boots.

Ms Malignus stopped in front of the children. She glared at them all. She hated them and she knew that they hated her. A thought that gave her deep satisfaction.

"Good morning, children," she said in a strong, guttural voice.

"Good morning, Ms Malignus," the children chimed monotonously.

"I trust that you are fully rested and that you are ready to work hard this week!" It was not a question. She looked around the room with disdain. "As you know, this school values discipline and academic success above all other things. I expect each and every one of you to carry on the good work of the school and to represent and uphold our good name and reputation." No one said a word. Ms Malignus stared hard at a young boy in the front row. Sophie could see that he was shaking.

"However, it seems as though some of you do not value this school as highly as I do." Ms Malignus paused for a moment. "You!" she screeched at the boy, pointing at him. "You in the red shoes. Come here immediately."

The boy didn't move. He didn't even look up. Like an eagle swooping down on its prey, Ms Malignus pounced on him, grabbing and hoisting him by his collar as she dragged him to the front of the hall. He looked terrified and was visibly shaking. She looked furious.

"What is this you are wearing?" she screamed at the boy. The excitement from the teachers was clear to see. One even started to clap like a seal. "These red shoes. Are they school uniform?" she bellowed. "Well, are they?" she yelled, shaking him by the collar.

"No, Miss," the boy squeaked.

"*No, Miss*," she mimicked, laughing in his face. Sophie noticed Mrs French licking her lips with her big fat tongue. The teacher with the blue shirt was visibly sweating and his grin had grown even larger. He was leaning forward in his chair, his eyes fixed upon the scene in front of him. All of the teachers had their eyes locked greedily on the young boy dangling under Ms Malignus's firm grip.

"No, Miss," she mocked again. "This is a clear example of not upholding the school rules, and damaging our good name." She bellowed across the hall, shaking the visibly terrified boy. All of the children kept their heads down, not watching what was happening. "Such insolence cannot and will not be tolerated," she spat out, shaking the boy once more. "There are consequences for such behaviour." The boy was now crying and had begun to try to squirm out of her grasp. He wriggled and tried to push her off him. His attempts were futile; she was far too strong and fast for him. She held out her finger and pressed it against his forehead. Immediately, he stopped struggling, and hung placid in her grip. "You will come to my office." She leaned in to the boy, close to his tear-stained face. "Naughty boys need to be punished." She smiled, whispering almost inaudibly.

"Now!" she barked loudly, "Assembly dismissed, return to your classrooms." She dragged the unresisting boy out of the hall. Sophie heard her footsteps echoing through the corridors. *Clack, clack, clack…* Quickly becoming quieter as she returned to her office.

One of the teachers stood up. He had a huge smile on his face, which was matched by the rest of his colleagues'. There was a clear excitement emanating from them all. He glared across the rows of children before motioning to his own class to stand up, following them as they silently left the hall. Each class of children quickly took turns to leave, followed by their excited teacher. Each leaving as quietly as they had entered. Some children continued to look down at the floor whilst others looked ahead, blankly.

Sophie was in a daze. *What on earth has just happened?* She had never seen a teacher behave like that before. She quietly walked alongside Penelope, back to her classroom.

5.

Sophie's head was spinning when she returned to her class. She was shocked at what she had just witnessed and couldn't exactly figure out what had happened. "Sophie," Mrs French called when they arrived back in their classroom, dragging her away from her confused thoughts. "I see that you are with me first lesson mmm, mmm." She was clearly very excited and seemed to be very happy. "You must go to see Miss Thomass in reception to collect your timetable. Penelope, you go with her. Make sure that she doesn't get lost mmm, mmm." She licked her lips and smiled.

Without saying a word, Penelope stood up and walked to the door. She stood waiting for Sophie.

"Yes, Miss," Sophie replied blankly, following Penelope. She was confused and unable to understand why the teachers all seemed so happy, considering what had just happened in the assembly. Surely they would have been upset and concerned about the treatment of that poor boy. She and Penelope walked out of the classroom together.

"What was all that about in the assembly?" Sophie asked when they were an appropriate distance from the classroom door. Penelope didn't reply and continued walking, staring straight ahead. "Penelope?" Sophie urged, pulling on the girl's arm. Penelope stopped and stared at Sophie for the first time.

"Talking is not permitted in the corridors. Thornberry Woods is an outstanding school." Her tone was flat and mechanic and her eyes seemed dull and lifeless. "Ms Malignus has turned this school around and created a marvellous learning environment. We are privileged to be here. We must respect the school values and follow the school rules at all times." With that, she quickly spun on her heels and resumed her journey to see the secretary. Sophie stood in silence, watching her walk away, amazed at how no one seemed to care or even be thinking about what had happened to the boy with the red shoes. She shook her head before hurrying to catch up. An uneasy feeling was beginning to grow in her stomach.

Miss Thomass was still perched on her seat, typing at the computer, as though she hadn't moved from when Sophie had seen her earlier. Penelope stood staring into the distance, waiting for her to look up. Both she and Sophie remained silent and after a moment or two Miss Thomass looked up and smiled at the two girls, revealing her rotten brown teeth.

"Yesss?" She immediately locked her yellow eyes on Sophie. Her greedy smile seemed to grow even bigger.

"Mrs French has sent us to collect Sophie Clearwater's timetable," Penelope recited.

"Of courssse," rasped Miss Thomass. She reached across to a stack of trays and lifted a sheet of paper from the top one. Her eyes never left Sophie. "Here you are, my dear." She held out the piece of paper, still grinning her rotten grin. Sophie tried to take the sheet but Miss Thomass held it tight. "Make sure you don't misss any lessonsss," she quietly hissed, "we like to know where you are throughout the day." She kept hold of the sheet. Sophie tried to pull it from her fingers but it didn't budge. Miss

Thomass raised her eyebrows. "I'm waiting," she said menacingly.

"Thank you, Miss," Sophie whispered, realising what she was waiting for.

"Good girl," said Miss Thomass, smiling and licking her lips. She let go of the sheet but kept her eyes locked on Sophie. "Now, back to classs you go."

Penelope immediately began walking. Sophie quickly followed her, glancing back once to see that Miss Thomass was watching them walk away. They walked in silence along the empty corridors. Sophie's head was reeling with the many unanswered questions she had but she already knew that Penelope was not the person who would answer them.

Penelope knocked on the classroom door before entering the room.

"Come in," chimed Mrs French. "Good, good, you're back." She waved the girls to their seats. Penelope sat down, immediately picked up her pen and began writing. "Let me see, let me see," Mrs French said excitedly. She waddled over to Sophie and looked at her timetable. "Good, good mmm, mmm," she muttered to herself, looking at the sheet. "Now, sit down and do your work. Copy from your book mmm, mmm." She handed Sophie her timetable back. "It is vital that you are in each lesson." She leaned in so close that Sophie could smell her foul breath. "We value academic success at this school mmm, mmm." She lingered slightly too long, making Sophie feel uncomfortable, smiling the whole time and showing those horrible pointed teeth. "Mmm, mmm," the teacher whispered, licking her lips before she waddled away.

That horrible uneasy feeling in Sophie's stomach continued to grow.

6.

Sophie tried to be as unnoticeable as possible for the rest of the lesson and made sure she did exactly what she had been told to do. She wrote, copying directly from her book, until her hands hurt. Occasionally, she glanced up to see Mrs French sitting at her desk, licking her lips and staring firmly right at her. Sophie quickly looked away, hoping that she hadn't been noticed, and along with her classmates continued to write furiously, her head down, hoping that the lesson would quickly finish.

When the bell eventually rang to signal the end of the lesson, Sophie began to get up from her desk, but no one else moved a muscle. She quickly sat down, hoping that she hadn't been spotted as Mrs French slowly and deliberately rose from her desk and looked across the room. She smiled at her class. "You may now leave. You have maths after your break with Mr Parkes mmm, mmm. Make sure you are not late." She licked her lips greedily. "Off you go now."

The children quietly put their books away and one by one filed out of the classroom. They walked sensibly and in absolute silence along the left side of the corridor, towards the oak doors and the outside yard. Sophie fell in line. She couldn't wait to get outside into the fresh air and some normality; even if the weather was grey, cold and miserable, it would be better than being stuck inside the uncomfortable warmth of the school. Maybe she could find someone who could tell her what was going on.

It was nice to be away from the stale, musty smell of Mrs French. Sophie was desperate to get away from Penelope too but being new to the school meant that she didn't yet have any friends she could go to. She needn't have worried about sneaking away from her, though, as the moment Penelope got outside she walked away, leaving Sophie completely alone, which suited her just fine. She took a deep breath, thankful for the fresh air, and had a look around the yard. She had expected to see lots of games being played and children running around, having fun, but she was surprised at the sight which greeted her. Three teachers were standing at different sides of the yard to each other, watching the children like vultures circling their prey. The sweaty one with the blue shirt was there, still smiling as he watched the children. An impossibly tall one was on the other side of the yard to him with a third teacher, who appearing to be more beard and hair than person, completing the triangle, standing under the stone archway. Between them, they could see every inch of the school yard.

A row of pupils, wearing little orange badges, had also taken positions around the yard. They were not talking to anyone and, like the teachers, they were watching the other children like hawks. These pupils and the three teachers had formed some sort of perimeter, surrounding everyone else on the yard.

"Weird," muttered Sophie to herself. There was no one running around anywhere; no ball games being played, or children chasing each other. There weren't any of the typical sounds you might hear on a school playground. No screaming, cheering or shouting. There were just small groups of children standing around quietly talking or sitting quietly reading or writing. The whole scene seemed to be incredibly organised and structured. Not at all what Sophie was used to.

The cold, wintry wind blew across the yard, Sophie shivered and began to walk around, trying to find someone to talk to, but all of them turned away when she drew near. Nobody would even look at her and all of a sudden she felt incredibly lonely and vulnerable.

After a few moments had passed, she saw the girl with the short black hair, who she had made eye contact with in the hall during the horrible assembly. She was talking within a small group of children. Sophie took a deep breath. *It's now or never, Sophie*, she told herself, blowing out a breath of cold air before walking over. "Hi, I'm Sophie. I'm new here."

The girl with the black hair stiffened and stopped talking. She looked uncomfortably at the group she was with, who looked equally nervous. No one spoke and an awkward silence fell amongst them.

"Hi, I'm Sophie," Sophie nervously repeated.

"Not here. Not now. They're watching," replied the girl. "Leave us alone." She picked up her bag and walked away, followed by her friends. Sophie was left truly alone and feeling incredibly uncomfortable and upset. She walked away from the spot, trying her best not to cry.

"Who was that?" one of the boys in the group asked sternly. He was tall, with fair hair.

"I don't know," replied the black-haired girl, looking around, "Some new kid. Think she's in French's class."

"French? Poor thing!" said a small boy with short blond hair.

"She talks funny," one of the girls said, "I don't think she's from round here."

"Yeah, she does," replied the girl with the black hair. "I was looking at her in assembly, you know, trying to suss her out a bit. She saw me looking."

"That was daft," snapped the boy with the fair hair. "Seriously, what if she'd been one of them and you'd been caught?"

"Doubt it," replied the girl. "She's new, isn't she? She won't be one of them; not yet, anyway."

"I don't know. French is quick!" he snorted back at her, clearly annoyed.

"Not that quick," she snapped back.

"So what are we going to do?" asked the smaller boy. He looked across with concern. "We can't just leave her to it, can we? She won't have a clue about this place."

"No. That wouldn't be fair," answered the girl with the black hair. "But we can't do anything now. It's too dangerous." They looked discreetly over at Sophie, who had sat down on a bench and was looking around the yard. She was shivering and rubbing her eyes.

"We've got to help her or at least warn her," whispered the small blond boy.

"I know." The girl with the black hair looked over at Sophie again, sharing the concern the others had shown. Just then, the bell sounded, to end break. The children began to line up, ready to go back to their classes. The girl with the black hair walked past Sophie and quickly whispered to her, "Lunchtime. I'll find you. Make sure you keep your head down and don't get noticed." Sophie stopped and watched her quickly walk away. She then became aware that she was being watched. One of the children with the orange badges was staring at her. Sophie quickly lowered her gaze and joined Penelope in their line. They quietly walked back into school.

7.

Sophie did exactly what the girl with the black hair had advised her to do and kept her head down during the next lesson. Mr Parkes was the hairy teacher she had seen on the playground. Close up, she could now see that he was the hairiest person ever. He had a huge beard, which was matted and thick, and he had thick, brown hair, which sprouted in all directions on his head. His skin was pale and flaky and he had the same stale and musty smell as Mrs French, although his was worse as he also smelt of dirt and grime, as though he had never washed or brushed himself before. All lesson, Sophie stayed quiet and worked from her book. She was polite and gave him no reason to even notice she was there in his class. She could, however, feel him staring at her.

Lunchtime seemed to take an age to arrive but when it did she quickly hurried out to the yard. She sat on the same bench she had sat on earlier and ate her sandwich. As she ate, she looked around and noticed that there were no teachers out in the yard at all. The students with the orange badges had taken their places around the perimeter as before but they seemed less watchful. As though they were tired and not quite switched on. Things out on the yard seemed to be a lot more relaxed. She could actually hear some of the children laughing and chatting, although in comparison to her old school it was still quiet and reserved.

The girl with the short black hair approached and smiled at her. She sat next to her on the bench and looked out at the yard, at the various groups of children. "What do you think?" she asked, not turning to look at her.

Sophie paused and thought about her answer. "It's weird."

"That's one way to describe it." The girl laughed quietly. "Is this your first day here?"

"Yeah."

The girl turned to face her for the first time and smiled. "Hi, I'm Lucy."

"Sophie," smiled Sophie.

"Come on, Sophie. Come with me and be careful not to be seen." Without saying another word, Lucy stood up and walked away. Sophie got up and followed her, making sure that she walked as calmly and sensibly as possible. Lucy walked to the edge of the yard, disappeared around the corner of the school building and waited for her to catch up. As soon as Sophie appeared around the corner, Lucy grabbed her by the arm.

"Quickly," she whispered.

At the back of the building were tennis courts, the school field, and an old, small wooded area. The tennis courts and field had once been the nuns' gardens but they had long been dug up and were now used exclusively for sports. The whole area was empty as Lucy started running towards the old wood, which was strictly off limits to all pupils. Sophie followed her, both of them running quickly across the sports field until they reached a large bush, which marked the edge of the wood. Lucy smiled breathlessly before grabbing Sophie by her arm and forcefully pulling her through the bush and in amongst the trees.

"Hey!" Sophie objected. "What are you doing? Where are we going?"

Lucy smiled at her. "Shh, you'll see," she grinned.

Without saying another word, the two walked deeper into the woods, following the line of the large brick outer wall that surrounded the entire school. They walked through the undergrowth for a short while until they came to a small, shaded clearing. The cleared area had thick bushes on all sides and was completely covered. It could not be seen from beyond the bushes, and could only be entered the way they had come in. The wind blew through the tops of the trees and the light peeped through small gaps in the branches above. Apart from the odd breeze, it was fairly well sheltered from the weather. A group of children came into view.

"Watcha, Luce," said a boy, looking up as she appeared. "You took your time."

"I've brought a friend," Lucy replied, pulling Sophie out from behind her. "Guys, this is Sophie. She's new, first day." She smiled. "Sophie, welcome to the Den."

Sophie looked at the small group of school children. There were three boys and four girls, sitting on a variety of logs, thick branches and seats, all salvaged from somewhere, eating their lunches. She recognised some of them who had been with Lucy earlier at break.

"Sophie, this is Jack, Boz and Ben." Lucy pointed to each of the boys. "This is Harry, Charlie, Kate and Claire," she said, indicating the girls. "Grab yourself a pew and make yourself comfy. You can relax and breathe easily here."

The others said their hellos as Sophie sat down carefully on a large branch next to Lucy.

"What is this place?" she asked.

"We've imaginatively christened it the Den," Lucy chuckled, "and we only come here at lunch." She smiled at

Sophie. "It's safer here than out there." Boz was glaring at her sternly. "Well, it is!" Lucy stated, glaring back at him. "Listen, Sophie," she said, her attention returning to the new girl. "Sorry about earlier; you know, at break. I didn't want to ignore you but you never know who is watching or listening."

"Never mind that," Boz interrupted, looking at Sophie. "Who are you?" He was the tall boy with fair hair who Lucy had been with during break. He was looking at Sophie incredibly seriously.

"You're the new kid in French's class aren't you?" Jack asked, shaking his head at how serious Boz was being and coming over to where Sophie was sitting. He was the short blond boy who had been with Lucy and Boz at break. He gave Lucy a wide smile.

"Yes," Sophie replied. "It's my first day."

"There you go, *Barry*," Jack said, turning to Boz and grinning at him. "She's a newbie so it's ok. Stop being so para."

Boz looked at him irritably and pulled a face, before grumbling something back at him. Jack laughed out loud.

"What do you mean it's safer at lunch?" Sophie asked Lucy.

"Surely you've noticed?" she replied, laughing. "They all lock themselves away in the staffroom… feeding." Lucy laughed, pretending to be a vampire and grabbing at Sophie.

"What she means is there are no teachers," Jack said, grinning at Lucy's vampire impression. He sat on the branch and squeezed in next to Sophie. "They never come out at lunchtime. Their 'Watchouts' are there but they're never quite as with it when there's no teachers around." He put his arms behind his head, still grinning at Sophie.

"Watchouts?" She asked, pushing Lucy off her.

"Yeah, the prefects. The ones with the orange badges. They keep a 'watch out' for the teachers and we 'watch out' for them." Jack laughed at his own joke.

"Hence, it's safer," Lucy took up the explanation. "Lunchtime is the only time you can never find a teacher; not that you'd want to, of course." Lucy smiled, taking a bite from her sandwich. "You said this place was weird."

"Weird?" gasped Harry, a small girl with dark-rimmed glasses and a tight ponytail. "It's more than that. It's horrible here. You're in French's class? You've seen what she's like? *Mmm, mmm*?"

"They're all like that," Lucy interrupted. "The teachers, they're all off. Something's not right about any of them. You know what I mean?" She looked at the others in the group for support. They all nodded and murmured in agreement.

"They go looking for you, trying to catch you breaking their rules," Boz said, staring into the distance, his face serious and grim. "When they find you…" He stopped speaking. A heavy silence fell over the group, lingering over them and Boz's unfinished sentence.

"That's enough of that, Boz," said Ben from across the clearing. He had long ginger hair, which fell in front of his eyes. "Leave it, eh?"

"It's her first day," Boz snapped back. "She needs to know. You've seen some of the kids here afterwards."

Sophie suddenly shivered, thinking of Penelope and Peter. "What happens to you?" she whispered.

"When they're found rule-breaking," Boz continued, "they change. They all change when they're caught." Sophie thought of the boy in the red shoes.

"In truth, we don't know what happens to them," Lucy said. "We just know they come out different. The teachers love catching the kids and sending them to Malignus." The others remained quiet. "You saw how excited they got in assembly, didn't you?" Sophie nodded. "That's why we couldn't talk at break. Couldn't risk getting caught. That's why we keep our heads down. Give them no reason to spot us." Lucy leaned back.

Charlie was sitting next to Harry and spoke quietly, "You've drawn the short straw coming here… I'm sorry." She began chewing her pigtails and gave Sophie an apologetic smile.

"Can't someone say something? If something is happening to the kids, can't we tell the parents?" Sophie asked, confused.

Jack laughed. "Tell them what? The teachers are horrible? Kids don't want to get told off? They're all good and well behaved after a visit to the Head's office?" He laughed and smiled sympathetically at her. "What would you say if your kids came home saying that?"

"All parents want their kids to behave and get the top marks, don't they?" Lucy asked, leaning in to Sophie. "Kids aren't supposed to like teachers and schools, are they? What would your parents say? I know mine wouldn't be that bothered if I started moaning about my teachers," she laughed.

Sophie looked at the floor, feeling foolish.

"Don't worry," said Claire, fiddling with her long blonde hair and smiling at Sophie. "We've all thought it. Besides, we don't know what happens. All we know is, they get sent to the Head and come back different … changed."

"Not us, though." Jack winked at Sophie. "You're one of us now and we'll look after you. Keep your head down and meet us here every lunch. You can have a laugh here with us."

Sophie smiled at him. "Thanks."

Lucy smiled, then looked sadly at her. "French is tricky. Watch out with her."

Sophie nodded and sat quietly whilst the others talked amongst themselves. "It's not all that bad," Ben whispered to her quietly. "Keep quiet, follow the rules and do the work, and you'll be fine."

"Work?" Sophie laughed, "All I've done is copy from books so far."

"Get used to it," he shrugged, "it's all we do. Still end up with top marks, though. Weird, eh?"

8.

That afternoon, Sophie sat in her lessons thinking about her new friends and everything they had talked about.

She was finding it hard to concentrate on her work as she had so many questions running around her mind. Why did the teachers become so excited during the assembly, and why were they all so smelly and strange-looking? What did Lucy and the others mean when they said the kids became different? What happened to them when they were sent to Ms Malignus? Why did her dad have to change jobs and send her to this horrible place? She didn't realise it but instead of working, as all of her classmates were doing, she was actually staring out of the window, lost in her own thoughts.

She was suddenly brought back to reality as she felt something hit her in the side of her face. Someone had thrown something at her. Panicking, she quickly looked down at her books and began writing furiously. After a few moments, she sneaked a look around the room to see who was throwing things. She noticed a boy with short black hair just behind her and to the side. He gave her a smile and pointed to his book, indicating that she should be writing. She smiled back at him. "Thanks," she mouthed.

The teacher at the front of the room made a strange snorting noise. Mr Fields was the geography teacher. He looked ancient, with wrinkly skin and long grey hair sprouting from his nose and ears. He was sitting behind his desk, his eyes wide open, staring into the distance. He made another snorting noise. *He's snoring!* Sophie thought. She glanced again at the boy, who was still looking at her. He stifled a small giggle and mimed someone being asleep before pointing at Mr Fields. Sophie quietly giggled and smiled back at him. Mr Fields suddenly coughed violently, waking himself up with a shudder. He immediately began looking around the room, as though he had never been asleep and needed to show it. Sophie and the boy quickly returned to their work.

When the lesson had finished, the children lined up by the door and began to walk quietly to the last lesson of the day. Sophie was walking in line behind Penelope when she felt someone tap her on the shoulder. She quickly turned to see it was the boy. Looking back at him, she blushed slightly. "Thanks," she whispered.

"It's ok," he whispered back. "Don't do it too often, though."

"Don't worry, I won't." She smiled at him.

"Talking is not permitted in the corridors," snapped Penelope, quickly turning to her side and staring at them both. "We must respect the school values and follow the school rules at all times."

Sophie quickly turned, facing forward again and following in line behind Penelope as they continued to walk to their class.

The next lesson was history with Mrs Atchison. She was a fierce-looking lady with small piggy eyes, a long chin and a large, hooked nose. She was tall and athletic-looking. Sophie immediately felt intimidated and slightly afraid. The room was cold and felt oppressive and tense. Sophie made sure not to daydream in this lesson, or do anything that might make Mrs Atchison notice her. She sat and wrote in her book until she felt as though she couldn't write anymore.

She thought she'd heard someone hiss at her, as though trying to get her attention: "Psst, psst," but she completely ignored it, not daring to risk getting caught not working by the vicious-looking teacher. When the lesson had finished, no one moved. The class must have sat silently for at least ten minutes. Sophie kept her face down but could feel Mrs Atchison's icy glare staring at her.

Eventually, the teacher allowed them to leave her room. Sophie slowly walked out, in line behind Penelope, keeping her gaze to the floor and doing everything to avoid the risk of seeing the teacher.

At last, she thought, *it's finished*. Her first day had been long and hard but it was finally over. The line of pupils walking out of the school towards the doors was moving far too slowly for Sophie but she daren't try and cut through it. Despite her desperation to leave the building, she did not want to draw any attention to herself by rushing now. *Come on, come on,* she thought as they finally reached the entrance and moved out onto the yard. She passed under the stone archway and walked calmly along the drive. The grey clouds had not yet given in to their threat of rain and the wind continued to blow the leaves across the path but the large iron gates were now in sight. She held her breath and calmly walked to them before eventually walking through them. *Yes*, she thought, breathing more easily, leaning against the large red-brick wall. *Is this to keep us in or others out?*

"Alright, Dolly?"

She looked up and saw the boy from the lesson looking at her and smiling. "Dolly?" she asked, immediately pulling her coat closed and pushing wisps of windblown hair behind her ear.

"Dolly daydreamer!" He smiled awkwardly at her lack of response. "Sophie, isn't it?" he eventually asked.

"Yes," she nodded. "Listen, thanks for before."

"No problem." He smiled, relieved to be moving on from his bad joke. "You'll get away with it with Fields after he's had his lunch," he grinned. "But maybe not some of the others." Sophie looked at him curiously. "I'm Tom."

"Thanks, anyway," she said, smiling. "He had his eyes open. How didn't he see me, and what was that noise he made?"

"He was snoring," Tom laughed. "He sleeps off his lunch but keeps his eyes open so no one notices."

The two of them started laughing together now.

"Don't do it again, though," he continued. "You were lucky Penelope or James didn't spot you." Sophie noticed a sad look come over him when he mentioned James' name, though it quickly disappeared. "Anyway, let's go before someone spots us and drags us back in," he grinned. "What way are you walking?"

"I'm not. I'm waiting for my mom to pick me up," she answered.

"Ok, then. Well, I'll see you tomorrow."

"Ok," she replied. He lingered a few more moments, looking unsure what to do. They smiled nervously at each other, an awkwardness hanging in the air, when a red car pulled up beside them.

"See you then," Tom laughed, the arrival of the car making his mind up. "And make sure you get a good sleep. Daydreaming is not allowed in this school," he mocked.

Sophie smiled and got into the car. She watched him walk away.

"Good day, honey?" her mom asked as she pulled the car out into the road.

"Yes," Sophie replied. She wanted to tell her everything Lucy and the others had told her, and about all the questions she had. But she remembered what Jack had said and realised he was right. Her mom would just think she was a kid who didn't like her new school. "It was good thanks," she lied as they drove away.

9.

Ms Malignus was exactly how she liked to be. Alone. She hated being with or around others – especially children – and she loathed the fact that she had been given a place such as this. She was lost in her thoughts as she sat at the large oak desk in her dimly lit office, her bony fingers steepled together in front of her face to form an arch just below her long, pointed nose.

Keeping the balance in the school was so important but it was becoming more and more difficult to do. She looked down at the half-filled glass on her desk. The thick, reddish-brown liquid within it seemed to shimmer in the hazy light of the room. She picked up the glass and took a long, slow drink from it, shuddering slightly as she swallowed. This is why she was here. This was their nectar, the 'Sanguine' that sustained them all. But appetites were growing and the directors at the academy were demanding she produce more and more. She knew the situation was the same with the other schools across the Academy; there simply wasn't enough Sanguine being produced but that didn't matter to her. The other schools were not her responsibility. She growled at the thought of the directors, sitting in their offices, safe and secure whilst she risked everything. It was she who took the Sanguine; she who had to endure the daily interaction with the children; she who had to keep the undisciplined animals in line and it was she whose head would fall if they were caught. She knew the

Academy would deny all knowledge of her activities and that she would be cut loose and made to take the blame for all of it. She longed for the day when she could leave this school; her prison, and take her rightful place on the high council.

A knock on her office door pulled her from her thoughts. "Enter," she called as imperiously as she could. She didn't hide the disdain on her face at the figure who entered the room.

"It is time, Headmistress," rasped the small teacher who had entered. "All of the children are gone." He avoided looking at her but his eyes kept shifting to the large oak cupboard in the corner of her office.

She hated him, as she hated them all. With the exception of a few elders, males were of a significantly lower caste than females and none were permitted seats on the high council. She quietly snarled as she watched him. Noticing the hint of greed on his face, her lip curled with annoyance. Her teachers were becoming more and more of a hindrance of late, becoming greedier and more bestial, yet she had no choice than to use them to help with the harvest. She was better than them, a higher caste, and hated having to associate with them at all, especially in matters so crucial to the Academy.

"I will be with you all presently. Wait for me in the staffroom," she snarled at him, annoyed at his presence in her office.

·"Yes, Headmistress." He slowly backed out of room, only looking up at her momentarily as he closed the door.

She picked up the glass again and swirled the contents within before finishing the drink, draining and savouring every last drop. She then opened a thin hidden drawer in her desk and removed a small golden key. She walked over to the oak cupboard and unlocked it, before stepping inside and closing the door behind her.

10.

*T*hat evening, Sophie lay in bed and thought of the events of her first day. It was safe to say that she didn't like the school yet. Sure, she had made some friends… was it too early to be calling them friends? But something was wrong with the place.

Her mom and dad had asked how her new school was over dinner and she had tried to talk to them about how she was feeling but they only wanted to hear what they wanted to hear, so she mumbled something vaguely positive and saved them from her negative thoughts. But what was it about the place that she didn't like? The teachers were odd; some of them were pretty gross, and the incident in the assembly left her with a nasty feeling but that wasn't it. She sighed and told herself off. It was an outstanding school; Penelope had told her that enough times, and part of an outstanding Academy. Maybe she was just having typical 'new school' thoughts. She rolled over and thought of Tom. He was quite cute and seemed nice enough. She smiled to herself and pulled the covers up over her head, hoping she would quickly drop off. *Tomorrow's a new day, maybe it will be better?*

The fact that it was still dark when she woke the next morning didn't help her mood. The uneasy feeling in the pit of her stomach had returned and she really didn't want to go to school.

"You'll be fine," her mom said, brushing aside her complaints about having to go in. "It's just a bit of anxiety. You'll get over it." They left and drove in silence the entire way, only speaking when they had pulled up outside the school gates to drop Sophie off. "Have a nice day." Her mom leaned over and gave her a kiss.

"Thanks, Mom," Sophie answered, kissing her back.

"You'll be fine, sweetheart, just wait till you've been here a while. Everyone says it's a good school and everyone takes time to settle in." Her mom smiled at her. "Anyway, it looks like you've made a new friend already," she teased, seeing Tom leaning on the wall and waiting for Sophie. "Isn't he the boy you were talking to yesterday, after school?"

Sophie felt her face flushing with embarrassment. "Leave it, Mom," she insisted, getting out of the car. "See you later." She smiled before walking over to the gates then waited and watched her mom drive away.

"Morning," she said to Tom as she walked over. She stood in front of the gates and looked at the old school. "Do we have to go in?"

"Afraid so," he answered, walking through the gates with her. He smiled, "It gets easier, though."

She didn't reply.

As they walked, Sophie felt that familiar feeling. She walked with Tom along the drive, neither of them speaking until they passed through the stone arch. The clouds weren't quite as grey but there was still a wintry chill in the air and the leaves were still dancing in the wind. The hush of the school yard made her feel uneasy. She looked across and saw Lucy with the others, talking quietly. Sophie walked over with Tom following.

"Hi, guys." She smiled at Lucy.

"Sophie," Lucy smiled back. "Survived your first day, I see?"

"Just," Sophie laughed.

"Alright, Thomas," smiled Jack. "Long time, no see."

Sophie noticed Boz giving Tom a disapproving look.

"Jack," Tom replied, giving him a nod. He looked at Boz. "Alright, mate?"

Boz didn't reply but gave a small, curt nod of his head and looked away. There was an uncomfortable silence.

"Come on, Soph, the bell's about to go," Tom smiled at her.

"I'd forgotten you were in French's class," Lucy said, looking at Tom, suddenly very serious. "You make sure you look after her."

Sophie grinned, "I can look after myself, thank you." She laughed.

Lucy smiled at her. "See you at break."

Having endured registration with Mrs French, Sophie's first lesson was Art, with a teacher called Mr Dalty. As they had done yesterday, the class walked in single file, quietly and sensibly, to the lesson. When they arrived, Sophie recognised Mr Dalty as the sweaty teacher she had seen the day before. She walked into his room behind Penelope and was immediately hit by an incredibly bad smell. The odour made her want to retch.

"Breathe through your mouth," Tom whispered as they walked into what felt more like a sauna than a classroom. The windows were all firmly closed and the radiators turned up full, too hot to touch. Sophie felt as though she would pass out.

Mr Dalty grinned at them all. He was wearing the same blue shirt he had worn yesterday, the sweat stains still visible and small beads of sweat now dripping from his head onto the shirt, making new stains. They were shown a picture and told to copy it. Mr Dalty hovered around the room, taking turns to lean over them to see their work. Sophie noticed that neither Penelope or James seemed bothered by the heat or the smell of Mr Dalty; they both continued to simply look ahead, staring into the distance. A few of the other children turned their faces away when he got too close to them. In fact, it seemed as though Penelope and James didn't appear to be even looking at their work whilst they were doing it.

"What have we here? A new child?" Mr Dalty asked quietly as he leaned in to look at Sophie's work. His voice was incredibly soft and he almost seemed to whisper into her ear, pronouncing each and every letter sound. A shiver ran down Sophie's back as he leaned in to look at her book.

"Let me see," he whispered. He grinned at her, leaning in so close that she could see crusty bits of sleep in his eyes. He was horribly pale and his grin seemed to grow even bigger, showing blunt, yellow stumpy teeth. He was so close that Sophie could see bits of food stuck between them. Combined with the heat and the rancid, putrid smell emanating from the man, it made Sophie start to physically gag. "Good, good," he grinned, his smile becoming even broader. He lingered slightly too long looking at her work before eventually moving on.

"I thought you were going to be sick. Right there on the desk," laughed Tom as they walked onto the yard at break.

"So did I," Sophie replied with a shudder. "How foul is he? Absolutely disgusting," she said, still feeling ill.

They saw Lucy and the others standing quietly as a small group on the yard and walked over to them. Lucy took Sophie by the arm and led her away from the others, whilst Tom watched on as they walked away. Sophie began telling her about Mr Dalty and his art lesson. "Mmm," she replied distractedly.

"What's up, Lucy?" Sophie asked.

Lucy paused then turned to look at her. "You and Tom?"

"Me and Tom?" Sophie laughed, feeling slightly embarrassed, "There is no me and Tom."

Lucy gave a concerned smile. "Just be careful with him."

"Why? What do you mean?"

"He's not careful enough," Lucy warned. "He's too risky and pushes it too much in front of the teachers."

Sophie smiled at her. "He's ok, he's just normal. Like you and the others, and I've not seen too much normal since I've been here."

"Just watch out with him, ok?" Lucy insisted.

"Fine," Sophie said, "but you don't need to worry. It's fine."

Lucy smiled at her but the look of concern remained. They walked back to the others, who were now all standing silently.

Lucy immediately became even more tense and concerned. "What's happened?"

"Look over there," Boz replied, indicating something behind her. Both Lucy and Sophie immediately looked around. The boy from the assembly was standing in the middle of the yard.

"Is that…?" Sophie began to ask.

"Yeah."

Sophie looked at him. He seemed pale and was gazing straight ahead, staring into the distance. He seemed to be dazed and slightly confused. Something seemed to be very different about him. She noticed that he wasn't wearing his red shoes anymore and was now in an immaculate school uniform, with a small orange pin attached to the lapel.

"Look at him," Lucy said.

"He shouldn't have got caught," Tom whispered. Sophie turned to face him and saw that he wasn't looking at the boy on the playground; the one that had caught the rest of their attention. He was looking at something else. Someone else. He was looking straight at James. The boy from their class.

11.

Tom seemed withdrawn. Sophie tried to get his attention several times during the next lesson but when Mr Parkes nearly caught her, she decided it was best to leave it and speak to him during lunch. After all, he was the only friend she had in the class.

When they were told to line up, she waited until Penelope had gone to take her place in the queue then made sure she was behind Tom in the line.

"Tom… Tom…" she whispered, trying to get his attention as they were walking down the corridor. "Tom," she called in the loudest voice she dared but he ignored her every time.

When they got outside, she pulled him back by the arm. "Tom, why are you ignoring me?"

"What?" he answered, looking confused.

"You've been ignoring me all lesson," she said. "Parkes nearly caught me trying to get your attention."

"Oh, I'm sorry," he replied. "I was miles away."

"What's up?"

"Nothing." He smiled at her. "Honestly, there's nothing wrong."

She didn't believe him but decided that there was no point pushing him any further with it. A short, uncomfortable silence fell between the two of them. The clouds above had dispersed to reveal a lovely, sunny winter's day. Sophie had an idea, which she thought might help Tom to open up a bit more with her.

"Come with me," she said, determined to help him.

"Where to?"

"You'll see." She smiled. "Follow me … but make sure no one sees you." She looked over at the Watchouts, as Jack had called them. She noticed that just as the day before, they didn't seem to be as alert as they had been during break. She turned and walked towards the corner of the school building. Tom shook his head and followed her, taking care to make sure that he wasn't seen by anyone. She waited for him to appear round the corner and as he did she took his arm and pulled him along. "Come on, we don't have all day," she laughed at him, pulling towards the school field and leading him towards the small wood at the back of the school grounds.

"Where are we going, Lucy?" he asked as she pulled him along. This time it was her turn to ignore him. She chuckled as she led him into the woods. She pulled him into the large bush that Lucy had dragged her into and, keeping against the red wall, they moved deeper and deeper into the growth.

"Where are we going?" he quietly hissed at her.

She laughed. "You'll see." She looked around, trying to remember the path Lucy had led her along the previous day. "You'll just have to trust me." Just as Lucy had done with her, she led him through the small wood until they came to the Den. Small spots of the winter sunlight dappled the area. No one else was there yet.

"What is this place?" Tom asked, looking around the clearing.

"It's great, isn't it?" Sophie replied, sitting on a branch and getting her lunch out of her bag. "Lucy brought me here yesterday. No one else knows about it."

"Lucy?" Tom asked, looking uneasy.

Sophie heard the voices of the others coming through the thick growth. Tom walked over to her and watched the entrance warily. Lucy appeared, followed by Jack. The others' voices weren't far behind. Lucy was laughing at something Jack had said but stopped when she saw Sophie and Tom.

"Hi, Lucy," Sophie called, looking happy and pleased with herself.

Lucy didn't reply but looked straight at Tom. The smile had left her face. "Tom!" she exclaimed. He looked at her awkwardly.

"What is he doing here?" shouted Boz, crashing through the entrance. His face was furious.

"Boz," laughed Sophie. "I thought I'd show Tom…"

"You thought?" he interrupted, his voice raised.

"Don't you shout at her," snapped Tom.

Sophie was confused and looked at Lucy as if to ask what was going on.

"You shouldn't be here," Boz threatened Tom.

"Don't worry, I'll go!" Tom stared angrily at Boz before starting to walk out.

"No, Tom," Sophie cried, angry now herself. She turned to Lucy. "Lucy, what's the problem...?"

Boz grabbed Tom by the shirt to drag him away. "Get out!"

Tom pushed him away. There was an awkward stand-off between the two boys, both glaring at each other. Suddenly, Boz launched himself at Tom, knocking him to the floor. The pair rolled around, punching and grabbing at each other. Jack and Ben quickly pulled them apart. Tom shrugged Ben off him and stormed away without saying a word, knocking past Katie and Claire, who were just turning up.

Boz looked at Lucy furiously. "You shouldn't have brought her here," he shouted, pointing at Sophie. "Look what she's done."

"It wasn't Sophie's fault!" Lucy shouted back at him.

"Just get her out!" Boz snapped.

Sophie was nearly in tears. Everyone else was silent.

"Boz?" Sophie pleaded, upset and confused.

"Just get out!" he spat at her, full of anger. Sophie did as he said, her face running with angry, confused tears.

"Well done!" Lucy snapped at Boz before running out after her. "Sophie!" She called. "Wait."

Lucy pushed her way through the bushes and trees, following the length of the wall. After a moment, she stopped and listened. She could hear crying. "Sophie," she hissed. The crying stopped. "Sophie, it's me." She moved further forward until she saw Sophie sitting on a log, wiping tears from her face.

"Hey," Lucy said, moving close to her friend. "Are you ok?"

"What was all that about?" Sophie asked through the tears.

"Yeah, sorry about that," Lucy replied. "Boz was out of order."

"What happened?"

"Just the boys being idiots." Lucy started to stroke Sophie's hair, pulling it back out of her face.

"Lucy," Sophie snapped irritably, pulling away from her. "No, it's got to be more than that. Boz really went for Tom."

Lucy looked at her, unsure what to say or do. After a moment, she sighed and gazed out into the woods, thinking hard about what to say.

"You're right," she said, fumbling for the correct words. "It was about Tom. Him and Boz, well, they just don't get on."

"I can see that," Sophie snapped. "But why? What's Tom done to deserve that? What's gone on between them?"

Lucy continued to look away uncomfortably.

"Please, Lucy," Sophie begged. "Tom's my only friend in that class. What's gone on?"

After a short silence, Lucy looked back at her. "It's about James Crew."

Sophie looked at her confused. "He's in my class, isn't he?"

Lucy just nodded.

"He's a prefect," said Sophie.

Lucy sighed. "Boz never used to be so serious, you know. He used to be quite fun." She looked at Sophie sadly. "He, Tom and James used to be really good mates. They went everywhere together and were always doing daft things. You know; messing about and trying to have a laugh. God knows you need to in this place." Sophie nodded at her, not saying a word as Lucy continued. "Well, the daft things became dafter, and they started to dare each other to do stuff. It started off small, you know, like pinching one of the teachers' pens, or writing on the desks and walls. Nothing harmful, really; just a bit stupid. As long as they didn't get caught, it was alright, and they never got caught."

She looked at Sophie. "You've got to understand that this was a couple of years ago, when we all first came here. This place has always been horrible but back then, we were younger. We didn't know how bad it could be, or what would happen. Anyway, the dares started to get bigger and more dangerous, each of them trying to outdo the other. They started flooding the toilets and setting off the fire alarms, you know, that sort of thing. You could see it was driving the teachers mad. They were furious about what was happening but they had no idea who was doing it, so couldn't stop it. We all thought it was hilarious. The boys had each other's backs and kept lookout for each other, so they were never caught. Anyway, Tom loved it. He really seemed to be enjoying secretly getting one over on the teachers but the other two weren't so keen. It was getting more and more serious and the teachers were getting really nasty, you know? Taking it out on everyone else because they couldn't punish the actual children who were breaking their precious rules. Boz wanted to stop but Tom didn't. I think James wanted to stop too but Tom kept going on and on at them to carry on. Tom dared James to sneak into the staffroom and set fire to a bin. Boz went mad, saying it was going too far, it was no longer just a prank. James didn't want to do it but Tom kept calling him names and egging him on. He wouldn't let it go."

Tears began to fill Lucy's eyes. She wiped them away and carried on. "One day, we were in class and all of a sudden we were marched into the hall. Malignus was already there, waiting for us. She had James, holding him by the collar. I've never seen anyone look so frightened. Boz and Tom were both white as sheets. We didn't know at the time but James hadn't gone to his lesson and had gone on his own to the staffroom to do the dare. Malignus was loving it; dragging him all over the place, she was. Like she was parading him in front of us all. The teachers were loving it, too. It was horrible, Sophie," she said, her eyes full to bursting.

Sophie shivered. The light under the trees seemed to lessen as the winter sun disappeared.

"Malignus dragged him away and, well, James is in your class; you've seen what he's like now." She stared at

Sophie. "Boz blames Tom and has never forgiven him for it. He's had nothing to do with him since," she sniffed. "But he shouldn't have gone off at you like that. He's alright really but, well you know…"

Both girls had tears in their eyes but Lucy started to cry openly. "That's when we really knew something dodgy was going on in the school. James just changed completely overnight." She snapped her fingers, "Just like that, he wasn't the same. He wouldn't talk to us; he never laughed or smiled anymore, and just sat there, staring into space and spouting how lucky we are to be here. It just isn't right." She paused. "Ever since then, we've kept our heads down and followed the rules, not wanting to end up like James. Boz came across the Den not long after it all happened. I think it was mainly to get away from seeing James… and maybe Tom," she added with a quiet sniff, looking at the ground. "We've been going there every day since." She looked up, "I hate this school and the teachers. We all do."

Sophie looked at her, "So all of the prefects, the Watchouts…"

"Normal, naughty, bratty kids," Lucy nodded. "Just like me and you, until Malignus got hold of them and turned them into her perfect little zombie prefects."

"That's horrible," Sophie said, sniffing back her tears.

"I know, but what can we do?" Lucy asked. "Prefects always get top marks, they're always behaving and following the rules. A teacher's dream." She began mocking them. "*Thornberry Woods is an outstanding school, Ms Malignus has turned this school around and created a marvellous learning environment. We are privileged to be here.* They're all the same." She sat up and began to wipe her eyes then looked at Sophie and laughed at the tears streaming down her cheeks.

"Come on you," she said, suddenly like her old self, as if their conversation hadn't happened. "It's no good thinking about stuff like that. Let's get you straightened up. Newbies can't go into class looking like that." She smiled. "Being normal means something in a place full of freaks. Let's not stop being normal, eh?" She took Sophie's hand and led her back towards the school.

Sophie's mind was racing. *What exactly is it that happens to these kids?*

12.

They had PE after lunch. Sophie had wanted to speak to Tom immediately but as they were separated during this subject, she didn't get the chance. Tom went off with the boys to one side of the sports fields, while Sophie stayed with the girls on the other. The sun was shining, although it was still cold, and whilst she was pleased to be outside running around instead of stuck indoors copying from a book, she was frustrated because it was a double lesson and that meant that she would not be able to speak to Tom until the end of the day.

When the time came for Miss Betteridge, the girls' PE teacher (a hugely muscled woman who reminded Sophie of one of the male American wrestlers on TV), to dismiss the girls at the end of the lesson, Sophie knew that she would have to move as quickly as possible if she wanted to catch Tom before he left.

"Tom," she shouted, seeing him walking through the archway. She was desperate to catch him but didn't want to draw attention to herself. She knew she couldn't run and didn't want to risk shouting again so walked as quickly as possible across the yard. As soon as she got through the arch, she began running along the drive. "Tom, wait," she called before catching him up and grabbing his arm.

"I don't want to talk," he said, shrugging her off without looking at her, then walking away.

"Tom, I know," she called after him, "I know about James." He stopped walking and turned to look at her. She could see how upset he was.

"Who told you?"

"Lucy. I tried to find you earlier, in the woods, after what had happened, but you'd gone. She found me and told me everything."

"So," he sniffed, "you'd probably be better off staying away from me as well then, wouldn't you?" He turned and began to walk away again.

"Don't be like that," she said, calling after him, "it's not your fault."

He turned around quickly and snorted a laugh at her, "Not my fault?"

"No."

"Then whose fault is it, eh?" he said angrily, walking towards her. "He'd never have done that if I hadn't dared him to. If I hadn't goaded him into it. It's all my fault."

Sophie took his hand in an attempt to calm him and try to offer some comfort but he pulled it away sharply. "Who put him in that position, eh? Who wouldn't let him back down from the dare?" He looked back up at her, his face a mixture of anger and guilt. His nostrils flaring and his jaw clenched. "I watch my best mate walking round this place like a zombie. He doesn't speak to me, he doesn't recognise me, it's like the James I knew doesn't even exist anymore; like it's someone else with his face on. Every single day, all of the time, and it's because of me. All of it." Tears filled in his eyes. He wiped them away.

"Tom…" Sophie whispered, trying to console him. She stepped closer to him.

"Yeah, that's right. Me." He snapped, "Maybe you'd be better being like Boz and staying away from me." He turned away from her and stormed off through the iron gates, leaving her standing alone at the top of the drive under the large oak trees. She ran up to the gates and was about to go after him when she heard a car horn sound. She looked to see her mom waving to her from the car, which was parked across the road. She watched Tom walking away.

"Alright, love?" her mom asked when she got into the car. "Sorry but I couldn't help but notice your argument with that lad. What was all that about?"

"Nothing," Sophie answered, pulling the seatbelt around her and avoiding her mom's gaze. "Just an argument between two of the boys. It happened at lunchtime."

"Nothing serious, I hope?" her mom replied as she started to drive away.

Sophie watched Tom walking along the pavement as they drove past him. Even though his head was down she could still see him wiping away his tears.

"Mom, why did you send me here?" she asked, turning to face her mother.

"You know why. We had to move because of your dad's job."

"Yeah, but why here?" Sophie persisted. "Why this school?"

"Well, it's supposed to be a really good school," her mom answered, not taking her eyes away from the road. "It got an outstanding inspection report and always gets the top marks in exams. Why do you ask? Do you not like it?"

"Not really. It's a strange place, Mom. The teachers are all horrible. They smell awful and they're really weird. Plus, all the work is boring, all we do is copy from books."

Her mom laughed continuing to watch the road and not once turning to look at her daughter. "I'm sure it's just because it's all new. You'll soon get used to it. Besides, don't all teachers smell?" She chuckled to herself. "I remember my old maths teacher, now what did we call him?" She began laughing, "That's right, it was Billy Bad Breath…"

Sophie switched off as her mom droned on about her own school days. Jack and Lucy were right. Parents wouldn't listen, and weren't any help.

13.

Tom became distant after that. As the term dragged on, and despite her best efforts to get his attention, he refused to speak to Sophie and completely ignored her. Boz was also ignoring her during break times, and whenever she went to the Den at lunch. He made no secret of the fact that he didn't want her there and she felt that if it weren't for Lucy or Jack she wouldn't have any friends in the school at all.

"Don't worry about him," Jack said one lunchtime in the Den. "He's just a moody git. He'll come around eventually."

"Yeah," Lucy agreed, "besides, it's not his wood, or Den. Technically, none of us are supposed to be here anyway, so don't you be paying him any attention. You come here whenever you want to. Me and Jack like having you around, don't we, Jack?" She punched him in the arm.

"Not if it means you'll keep hitting me," he laughed, pushing her.

Sophie smiled at them both. She was pleased to have their friendship but still worried about Tom. She would watch him walking around the yard on his own during break and could never find him at lunchtime.

"Leave Tom," Lucy suggested one day when Sophie mentioned her concerns. "I told you to watch out with him."

"I know," Sophie replied, "but I feel sorry for him. He blames himself for everything and he shouldn't."

Lucy shook her head. "Maybe, maybe not, but Tom's the one who took it too far, isn't he?" she answered firmly. "Even if James hadn't been caught, he'd have just kept pushing it." Sophie tried to interrupt her but Lucy wouldn't allow it. "No, Soph, you've got to listen. Daring someone to set fire to things is seriously messed up. Who thinks that sort of thing is funny?" Sophie didn't answer. "Exactly!" Lucy continued, taking her silence as an agreement. "He's bad news, is Tom. Stay away from him." Sophie didn't respond and kept her feelings to herself.

The weeks leading to the end of the term crept slowly forward. The only thing that kept Sophie going was the time spent with Lucy and Jack. She continued to feel unsettled by the teachers, who all gave her the creeps, whilst all of her lessons continued to drag on and bore her completely. Nevertheless, she kept her head down in the classroom and followed all of the school rules, to avoid any and all teacher interaction or attention. But despite Lucy's and Jack's warnings, she still found herself worrying about Tom. She had even tried to talk to her parents about him and the school, and tried to tell them about all the worries and concerns she had, but they just dismissed everything she had to say.

"Sophie!" her dad would respond whenever she mentioned the school or her teachers. "You're not changing school, so stop with this nonsense and get on with it. Honestly, I expect more from you."

"He's a teenage boy," her mom would say whenever she mentioned Tom, "I'm sure he'll come around." More often than not, she would then go on to make some sort of comment about changes and hormones. Sophie felt as though she had no one she could talk to.

On the final day of the term, Sophie was walking down the corridor towards their last lesson of the day: Geography, with Mr Fields. It had been a pretty miserable day and she was looking forward to a few weeks away from the place. Tom was still ignoring her and Boz's moody attitude and filthy looks were making her feel less and less welcome. To make things worse, she hadn't seen Lucy on the yard or in the Den that day and, as much as she liked being with Jack, he really couldn't replace Lucy.

Sophie traipsed slowly in line towards Mr Fields' classroom, and noticed that she happened to be behind James. As she looked at him, an idea began to form which she thought could help everyone.

When they entered the room, she sat down and took out the textbook that she knew they would be copying from. Making sure that nobody could see her, she carefully ripped out several pages of text. She looked again to double check that no one had seen her do it then noticed Tom looking at her, his eyes wide open. He gave her a quizzical, concerned look but she turned away, completely ignoring him. She waited until the lesson had begun before approaching Mr Fields at his desk.

"Who said you could stop working?" growled the teacher, shocked to see someone coming to speak to him during the lesson.

"Sorry, sir," Sophie replied. She was nervous but tried not to show it on her face. "I was wondering if I could go to the library to get a replacement book? You see, my book is missing several pages." She showed him the book she had ripped the pages from. She could see the anger growing inside the teacher.

"This is most irregular," he snarled. "Go quickly and get your book, then come straight back here." She stood still, looking at him. "Hurry, girl," he snapped. "Don't try my patience."

"Please, sir," she asked nervously, "I'm new here and I'm still unsure of the school. I don't know exactly where the library is. Could I ask for someone to show me?" Mr Fields looked both confused and angry. He was clearly flustered by the request and wasn't used to anyone even talking to him during his lessons, never mind asking to leave the room.

It's now or never, thought Sophie, swallowing hard. "Could James please show me, sir?" she asked before quickly adding, "He's a prefect and would ensure that I don't get lost and can quickly return to class."

Mr Fields was rapidly losing his patience with this interruption and wanted it over. He bristled and looked at her menacingly. "Very well, girl." He growled, "You have ten minutes to return with a new copy of the book or else…" He left the threat to hang in the air. "James Crew," he called out to the room, "take this girl to the library. Ensure that you are back within ten minutes." He looked at Sophie, full of malevolence, then grinned menacingly at her. "Go."

James quickly left the room without saying a word. Sophie followed him, surprised at the speed they were walking. "James," she called him, trying to get his attention. "James…"

"Talking is not permitted in the corridors," he responded, not turning around or slowing his stride at all.

"James, I need to talk to you." Sophie was almost jogging to keep up with him. He didn't respond but turned a corner and led her through a door into the library.

Sophie was amazed at the size of the room. The walls were all covered in books, rows upon rows of them, and in the middle of the room were great big shelves which were filled with books of different sizes and thicknesses. There appeared to be no tables to work on, however; only a large desk directly opposite the door they had walked through. Sophie cautiously approached it. Behind the desk sat a small woman, barely bigger than the desk itself, with small, round glasses perched upon the end of her nose and a tight grey bob on her head. Sophie's heart was racing as she approached. She quickly scanned the scene, noticing stacks of books and boxes containing various school items and stationery. Paperclips, orange prefect badges, and various stamps, pens and pencils. The small teacher was engrossed in a book and held her finger up, as if telling the children to wait, her eyes rapidly moving back and forth over its pages.

"Yes?" she said, eventually looking up from the book she had been reading and smiling at them. Sophie was shocked. She was the first 'normal' looking member of staff she had seen at the school and certainly the first one she had seen smiling.

"Erm, Mr Fields has sent me for a copy of our Geography book, Miss. The copy I have is damaged," Sophie replied. A look of anger flashed across the librarian's face but quickly disappeared.

"What a great pity, dear. Tell me what it's called and I'll go and fetch a replacement for you."

Sophie was completely thrown by how nice the librarian seemed. She held out her book with the missing pages. "It's this one, Miss."

"Ah, *Mountains, Rivers and Fields*," the strange librarian replied, looking at the book disappointedly, as if seeing a damaged copy upset her. "One moment, dear," she said before shuffling off to find it.

Sophie watched her walk away. "James," she whispered. He ignored her and just stared ahead blankly. "James," she continued, "talk to me. I need to talk to you, about Tom."

"Talking is not permitted in the library," he chanted.

"Please talk to me," she insisted, standing right in front of him and trying to break his stare and get his attention. "Tom is your friend. He's sorry and wants to be friends again." She had hoped that talking to him about Tom might help the two sort out their differences and become friends again. His expression didn't change, however.

"Talking is not permitted in the library," he repeated.

"James, talk to me, please, at least won't you talk to Tom?" she insisted. He continued to stare into space.

"Talking is not permitted in the library," he repeated mechanically.

Sophie looked at his lifeless expression. He continued to stare ahead, not even seeming to notice that she was there. She was crestfallen. She had thought that if she could speak to James, she might be able to convince him to talk to Tom. Apart from Penelope, it was the first time she had really spoken to a prefect, and she now knew what Tom had meant when he'd said James was like a zombie.

"Here you go, dearie," said the librarian, shuffling back to them and handing Sophie the book. She held her gaze, looking at her dangerously, making sure that Sophie understood what she was about to say. "This book is in pristine condition, please ensure it stays that way. Books are a vital source of our knowledge and of recording our history. They must always be respected and looked after." She then smiled again, "Hurry along back to class now, dear. Students must *always* be in their lessons."

James immediately turned and walked out of the door. The librarian smiled at Sophie as she quickly turned and followed him.

"Just in time," growled Mr Fields as they returned to class. He looked disappointed. "Sit down and get on with your work."

As she returned to her seat, Sophie noticed Tom staring at her angrily.

14.

"What the hell was that about?" snorted Tom, grabbing Sophie by the arm as she walked out of the school onto the yard.

"Get off me!" she snapped back, spinning around to confront him.

"What are you playing at, Sophie?"

The two stood and angrily stared at each other. Each just as annoyed at the other, neither of them speaking. Sophie turned and stormed away from him, pleased to be giving him some of his own treatment. She marched through the stone archway onto the long drive without looking back at him. Tom quickly followed her.

"That was a stupid idea, Sophie," he blurted out, "ripping pages out of your book and then going out of the lesson."

She turned sharply to face him. "Be quiet before someone hears you!" she hissed, stopping him in his tracks.

"Do you know how much trouble you could have got in?" he asked her angrily. "You shouldn't have done that!"

"What do you care?" she snapped back, just as angry. "How dare you tell me what to do when you've not spoken to me for weeks!"

"Doesn't mean you should be putting yourself at risk though, does it?"

"I'll do what I want!" she responded defiantly. They stared at each other. Neither wanting to back down but both wanting the row to finish. Tom looked at the floor, his stance softening.

"I'm sorry," he mumbled.

"You're what?" Sophie asked, still angry with him.

"I'm sorry," he sighed, slightly louder, "for ignoring you."

"So you should be!" she snapped before turning around and storming off again. He chased after her.

"Sophie, just stop a minute." She stopped but didn't turn around. He stood in front of her. "What were you doing?" he asked calmly.

She chewed on her tongue for a moment, quietly glaring at him. The anger she had was still clear on her face. "I was trying," she eventually huffed, "to sort out this mess between you and James. I thought that if I spoke to him and explained things then he might talk to you." She noticed a sadness creep over Tom's face when she mentioned his friend.

"I told you James is gone," he said quietly. "You should've left it alone."

"Well, I wanted to try," she answered. The skies darkened as drops of rain began to fall.

"And what if you'd been caught?" The exasperation suddenly returning in his voice. "Then you'd have ended up just like him, wouldn't you?"

"Oh, so all of a sudden you care now, do you? Weeks of nothing. Not even a hello, but now all of a sudden you care?" The tension was rising between the two of them once more. The rainfall became heavier.

Tom glared at her. "You don't get it!"

"Don't get what?" she snapped back.

"That what happened to James was because of me!"

All of the anger and hostility that had been so very present between them both suddenly disappeared. She edged closer to him, the rain falling heavy between them, and looked him straight in the face.

"Because of you?" she whispered, ignoring the downpour. "You're right. James is like a zombie but that's not down to you, is it?" Despite the weather, she could see the tears in his eyes. "Whatever happened to him is because of *them*." She jabbed a finger at the school, her tone softening. "It's because of this place, not because of you." She looked at him, hoping that her words would mean something. "It's not your fault, Tom."

For that brief moment, it seemed as if it were just the two of them, alone on the drive All she could hear was the rain pouring through the trees. Tom looked at her, tears in his eyes and a sadness in his face.

"You're right," he said softly. "It is because of them." His face hardened at the thought of the school and his friend. He stared at her, a determination lighting in his eyes. "Not anymore, though. It won't happen again." Sophie suddenly felt worried. Tom didn't appear to be looking at her but through her. "I'm going to find out what they're doing and stop them," he said.

"What do you mean?" she questioned him, her concern growing. "What are you thinking, Tom?"

"You'll see," he answered grimly before turning around and walking away, without another word. She stood in the rain and watched as he walked through the iron gates. The wind was beginning to pick up and the rain was even heavier but she didn't seem to notice. She had been looking forward to the end-of-term break but she wasn't so sure now; she wouldn't see Tom again until they returned to school and didn't know what he was planning, or what he might do in the meantime. She watched him walk away, a nagging doubt growing in her stomach.

"Just don't do anything stupid," she whispered as he disappeared in the rain.

15.

"Something's not right," Sophie said that evening, talking to Lucy on the phone. "Tom seemed really strange when he walked off."

"Maybe," Lucy replied, "but what were you playing at with Fields? Honestly, Sophie, anything could have happened to you."

"I know, but I had to try something." Lucy didn't respond. "So what do you think about Tom?" Sophie asked nervously, wondering how Lucy might reply.

"I think what I've always thought," she answered. "Leave him alone. He's not worth it." There was an uncomfortable silence. "He'll get you in trouble," Lucy continued. "Look at James…"

"That's not fair!" Sophie interrupted.

"Isn't it?" Lucy fired back. "First, James gets caught doing something stupid. Then you start acting stupid, too. And Tom is bang in the middle of it. Let him be, Sophie." This time, Sophie didn't respond. After what seemed like a long pause, Lucy finally spoke. "Look, I've got to go. My dad's shouting up at me to get off the phone. Promise me you won't do anything stupid, Sophie?"

"Like what?"

"Like anything… just promise me."

"Fine, I promise," Sophie eventually answered.

"Good. Now, very quickly, what are you doing tomorrow?" Lucy asked.

"Nothing. Why?"

"Come round to mine, we can do nothing together," Lucy laughed. Sophie laughed, too; it was nice to know their differences over Tom wouldn't come between them. "Ok, Dad, one more minute," Lucy shouted to her father then spoke back into the phone. "Are you coming?"

"Yeah… about twelve?"

"Twelve is great. See you tomorrow, then."

"Ok, see you tomorrow." Sophie ended the call.

That night, Sophie slept poorly. She couldn't stop worrying about Tom, what he was planning, and generally how off he had been with her.

"Seriously, Sophie, can we not have a break from talking about Tom?" Lucy moaned. Because the rain had stopped they had decided to go shopping. Sophie had brought up the subject again whilst they were having lunch.

"I'm just worried, that's all," she answered.

Lucy huffed at her and put her burger down on the table. The restaurant was noisy; a kid was having a party in the special birthday zone and there were children running all over the place. Lucy watched as a six-year-old with ketchup all over his face threw some fries at his friend. The child's mother didn't even look up from her phone.

"Look, would it help if we went round to his house?" Lucy asked. "Anything to get out of this place," she added grimly.

Sophie smiled at her and nodded. "Do you know where he lives?"

"I don't, no, but luckily I know someone who does. Come on." The two girls picked up their bags and the remainder of their meals. The child whose party it had been was now crying because one of his friends had eaten his burger. Lucy shook her head.

There was a gentle breeze as they walked through the village and it looked as though the spring sunshine was trying to break through the clouds. They talked about their plans for the school holidays. Lucy was going away with her family so wouldn't see Sophie again till they were back in school. Sophie's dad's new job meant that he couldn't have any time off work so they wouldn't be going anywhere. She didn't know what she was going to do.

Eventually, they reached the place they had been heading to. Lucy knocked on the door and a large woman with blonde hair and dangling ear-rings answered it.

"Hi, Miss Dahill. Is Jack in, please?" Lucy asked politely.

The woman smiled and shouted back into the house. "Jack, there's a couple of girls here to see you." She smiled at Lucy. Jack's head appeared in the hallway, behind his mom. He walked over to the door, looking curiously at Lucy.

"Alright, Lucy… Sophie," he said. "What's up?"

"What sort of welcome is that?" His mom laughed. "Honestly, Jack, have you got no manners?" Lucy and Sophie stifled a laugh as Jack blushed. "Come in, girls."

"Ok, Mom," Jack moaned. "Come in, guys."

His mom stepped out of the way whilst Lucy and Sophie walked in, smiling politely at her.

"Jack, I'm just off to the shops," his mom smiled as she put her coat on. "Do you guys want anything whilst I'm out? Some pickies or snacks, maybe?"

"No, Mom, we're ok!" Jack answered, giving her his best 'go away' smile. She chuckled at him and blew him a kiss before closing the door and walking out.

Jack rolled his eyes. "Sit down, guys," he said, leading the girls into the living room. "What's up?"

"Why should something be up, just because we've called round?" Lucy said, laughing. He smiled at her.

"Do you know where Tom lives?" Sophie blurted out. "Sorry, I'm just really worried."

"She hasn't mentioned him for a whole fifteen minutes." Lucy laughed. "It's a record."

Jack laughed too. "Why are you worried about him?"

Lucy and Sophie filled him in on everything that had happened.

Jack looked at Sophie and shook his head. "You're not going to listen to us, are you?" He asked looking concerned, "He's not worth it."

Sophie didn't answer. Jack looked at Lucy, who shrugged her shoulders. He huffed at them, "Ok then. I don't know his address but I know how to get there."

"Let's go, then," Sophie said, standing up.

"What, now?" Jack exclaimed.

"Yeah, now." She smiled at him.

The three walked through the village towards Tom's house. The spring sun had retreated behind the clouds but it was still a pleasant day. Jack led the way, messing around and trying to make the girls laugh.

"He likes to act the laidback joker," Lucy whispered to Sophie, "but under the surface there's a serious, more sensitive person itching to get out." Jack pretended not to have heard her.

After a while, they reached Tom's house. Sophie walked up the drive and knocked on the door, whilst Jack and Lucy stayed back on the pavement. She waited a moment before looking through the front room window and then knocking several more times but there was no reply.

"There's obviously no one in, Soph," Lucy called. "Leave it and come back tomorrow."

Sophie was about to give up when an old woman called from the house next door.

"Hello, hello! What are you lot doing?" She hobbled over, leaning heavily on her walking stick. "Who are you and what do you want?"

Jack turned away, stifling a laugh at how abrupt the old woman was.

"I'll have you know this is a neighbourhood watch area and we look out for each other."

"I'm really sorry to bother you but do you know if Tom is in?" Sophie asked politely.

"Who is it who's asking?" the woman asked, looking Sophie over suspiciously.

"We're Tom's friends from school," Sophie replied with a smile.

"Mmm, well the Bennetts aren't in," the old woman mumbled. "I'm keeping an eye on the place until they get back."

"Until they get back?" Sophie queried. "Does that mean they've gone on holiday or something?"

The old woman looked annoyed with herself. "It means, can I help you with anything?" she snapped.

"No, thank you," Sophie answered disappointed. "It was Tom I wanted to see but it can wait."

The old woman's eyes narrowed and she took a step closer to Sophie as if she was getting a better look. "Well I'm sorry, I can't help you there," she said, still sounding annoyed. "Now, if there's nothing else I'm sure you must be getting along." She gave a stiff smile and started to walk towards Sophie, almost forcing her away from the door. "I'll be sure to let them know you came by."

Sophie politely thanked the woman and walked back down the drive to Jack and Lucy. The old woman followed as quickly as she could, leaning on her stick. Jack finally let out his laugh as they walked away. He glanced back once to see the old woman was standing watching them, presumably to make sure they'd gone.

"Well, she was very pleasant," he said sarcastically. "*We are a neighbourhood watch area*." He mimicked.

"Well, that's that," Lucy said, laughing at Jack but turning to Sophie. She linked arms as they walked away. "You'll just have to wait until we get back to school."

"Oh, don't remind me of that place," Jack moaned, his mood quickly changing.

Sophie shrugged her shoulders and smiled in resignation. With no way of speaking to Tom, and with Lucy going away, she knew she was in for a frustrating and lonely time.

16.

The school holiday dragged. It rained almost every day and Sophie had spent most of it alone whilst her mom and dad were out at work. She couldn't remember how to get to Jack's house and without Lucy around she had no other friends to hang out with. She spoke to some of her friends from her old school on the phone but it wasn't the same as actually being there with them.

She found she was actually glad when the new school term finally started, but also incredibly anxious about what was happening with Tom. After two weeks of thinking and mulling over everything that they had talked about, she still had no idea what he was going to do. On the first day back, she made sure that she arrived as early as possible at the school and waited for Tom by the archway, thinking about how he'd seemed when they last spoke. She also thought about Lucy and all of the warnings she'd given her.

"Tom," she called excitedly, as she saw him walking along the drive towards her. "I've been worrying about you."

"Why?" he asked, looking at her apprehensively.

"Because of everything we'd said on the last day. You seemed really strange when you left. Is everything ok?"

"Yeah, it's fine," he said, walking towards her and smiling. "Listen, I'm sorry for ignoring you. I genuinely thought it was for the best but I was wrong." She smiled back. "I've got to run," he added quickly, "I'll see you in class."

Two whole weeks had passed and he hadn't even stopped to talk to her properly or ask how her break had been.

"Ok." She looked at him curiously, confused and disappointed at how eager he was to get away from her. She watched as he entered the school without once looking back.

By the time Sophie arrived in class, ready for registration, Tom had gone. She had followed him into the school but had quickly lost sight of him. She looked around the classroom, which was slowly filling with children coming in from the yard, but couldn't see him anywhere.

"Everyone sit down, mmm, mmm," Mrs French called to the class as she entered the room. "I hope you all had a restful break and are ready to work hard, mmm, mmm?" She smiled grotesquely at them all as she scanned the room. "Mmm, mmm we appear to be missing a child," she said, licking her lips slowly. Sophie watched as a gleeful look flashed across the old toad's face. "Being late is against the school rules, Ms Malignus will be upset mmm, mmm." She grinned widely.

Sophie couldn't help but worry. *Where are you, Tom?* A nervous feeling began to grow in the pit of her stomach.

Tom watched as the teachers left the staffroom one by one. He had managed to squeeze himself into an old mop cupboard, from which he could see the door to the room. When he was satisfied that all the teachers had gone, he carefully left his hiding place and snuck through the door.

He gagged from the smell as he entered the staffroom. It was like nothing he'd ever smelt before. Like a combination of rotten eggs and meat that had gone off. He held his breath and looked around him. The windows were grimy and greasy and let barely any light in. The carpet was tacky, like something had been spilt but not cleaned up. No one other than the teachers ever came into this room and he was disgusted at how filthy it was.

Other than the smell and dirt, however, it looked just as he would have expected it to. It had all of the usual furniture, cupboards and equipment that any other staffroom would have and there were working areas for the teachers, noticeboards full of information, and shelves full of files and books.

There was one cupboard, however, that was different to all of the others and looked out of place. It was an old antique oak cupboard, which sat closed at the far end of the room. Tom stared at it as though he had no choice. For that moment, he seemed to forget where he was and slowly walked over, mesmerised by it. He took hold of the door handle, which was horrible and sticky. The door would not move. He let go of the handle as though his hand had been burnt and suddenly all of his consciousness returned.

He looked around the room again. It was as though he had forgotten where he was, and how he had got there. A sudden dread crept over him and he quickly and cautiously left the putrid room to search elsewhere.

Sophie had expected Tom to turn up for registration. When he didn't, she began to grow increasingly worried about his safety and what he was doing. She had an idea.

It worked with Mr Fields so why not on her?

She approached Mrs French's desk.

"Excuse me, Miss?" she asked as calmly as she could.

"Mmm, mmm," replied Mrs French, seemingly irritated by the girl's approach. She looked at Sophie through her thin-rimmed glasses and licked her lips. Sophie wanted to retreat from the foul woman. Mrs French smiled at her and Sophie suddenly felt more fear of the woman than she had of Mr Fields. A panic began to flow through her.

"I'm sorry, Miss," she began, "but could I please use the toilet?"

An excitement appeared in Mrs French's face, as if in anticipation of some unknown treat. "Why didn't you go earlier mmm, mmm?" she asked, running her fat tongue over her sharp, pointed teeth.

"I did, Miss," Sophie replied meekly, swallowing hard, "but I have a water infection and need to go again."

Mrs French's smile disappeared and a look of disgust appeared on her face. "Very well," she conceded, "but only because there is a medical need." She almost spat out the words. "Make sure you go straight to the hall afterwards for assembly." She glared horribly at Sophie but then seemed to change as if a slow realisation had dawned upon her. "Don't be late though," she said, that grotesque smile returning to her face. "One child being late would require a punishment but two children, mmm, mmm." She looked away from Sophie and seemed lost in a blissful daydream.

"Thank you, Miss," Sophie replied, now even more worried but not just for Tom.

Mrs French waved her away with a short stubby hand.

Sophie left the classroom, determined to find Tom, to stop them both from getting into trouble and from being punished. But where could he be? Although she was getting better at finding her way around the school, Sophie still wasn't entirely sure of the layout. She crept around as quietly and as quickly as she could, looking for her friend, but she knew it wouldn't be long before the halls were filled with teachers and students on their way to assembly. She felt hopelessly lost, not knowing where to begin looking for him, and began to regret her decision. She thought about the warnings Lucy had given her and worried about what could happen if she was caught wandering around the school, especially given how perversely happy French had looked at such a prospect.

Accepting that she had no way of knowing where to look, she decided to give up and had begun to make her way to the hall when she saw him. He had just disappeared around a corner at the end of the corridor. Sophie quickly made her way to the corner and stopped when she saw where she was. Tom had just turned into a small alcove, halfway down the main school corridor. Sophie followed him into the corridor and towards the alcove, not daring to call his name, but froze as she looked into it. There was only one door at the end of the alcove and Sophie felt a shiver run down her spine when she read the name plaque hanging from it.

Ms V Malignus

Oh no, Tom, she thought, staring at the door.

Tom had gambled that the Head wouldn't be in her office but that she would be in the hall for the assembly. He put his ear against the door and knocked on it, ready to run at the slightest sound. Not a peep came. He slowly turned the handle, expecting the door to be locked, and was surprised when it slowly opened, brushing quietly against the carpet. He looked again to make sure nobody was watching before slipping quickly inside.

He closed the door and stood behind it, taking a long, deep breath. His heart was beating so loudly in his chest that he was worried it might be heard. He slowed his breathing and looked around the office. The windows and blinds were closed, leaving the room dark and gloomy, and there was a musty smell hanging in the air. The room looked pretty much as he'd expected it to, just slightly grander. In one corner, there was a large, expensive-looking antique oak table with a big leather chair behind it. There was a small coffee table with chairs surrounding it in the opposite corner and on the walls there were several shelves filled with tomes of ancient-looking leather books lined up neatly, one after the other. However, it was the large oak cupboard standing in the far corner that had Tom transfixed.

The cupboard looked antique, like it had been made centuries ago, and Tom couldn't take his eyes from it. It was similar to the one he had seen in the staffroom but grander and much, much older. He felt himself slowly being drawn towards it. There was a strange, eerie quiet to the room, as if all sound was being absorbed and digested within the space. Tom felt the wooden frame of the cupboard. It didn't feel like wood. It felt fuzzy and warm and soft, like an old suede coat. He couldn't explain why but he had to open that door. The urge was too compelling for him to resist and he tried to turn the handle but it was locked tight. He quickly looked around the room for something to jemmy the door with and from the corner of his eye noticed a small glint of flickering light. He looked over to its source and noticed a thin drawer, which slightly open, in the old oak desk. The drawer was so small and thin that had it not been open he would never have seen it. He carefully opened the drawer fully. It was completely empty, save for a single small golden key that glistened even in the gloom of the room.

Tom took the key and closed the drawer, leaving it slightly open so he could find it again and replace the key later. He walked over to the cupboard and carefully tried the key in the lock. He heard a click and then the creak of the hinges as the door opened slightly. Tom took the key out of the lock and put it in his pocket.

His heart nearly stopped beating when he opened the door fully and saw what was inside.

Sophie quickly walked over to the office door and put her ear against it. She couldn't hear a sound coming from the room. She put her hand on the handle, ready to follow Tom into the room, when she heard a noise.

Clack, clack, clack. It was getting louder. Closer. She had to go. She knocked three times on the door with her knuckle, to try and warn Tom, before quickly leaving the alcove and stepping out into the main corridor. Other doors were now opening as different classes began to make their way to the hall for the assembly. Sophie quickly joined one of the lines, following them to the hall, and prayed that Ms Malignus, or anybody else, had not seen her. She could only hope that Tom had heard her knocking. He was now on his own.

17.

*T*om stood unblinking, staring into the cupboard. He could barely understand what he was looking at. He had expected to see shelves filled with books or files; the kinds of things that anyone would expect to see in any office cupboard. What he was looking at was much stranger. Instead of shelves, there was a long flight of stairs, leading down into nothing but darkness. Tom stood still, barely breathing, completely transfixed by the stairwell and where it might lead, when he heard a noise. He turned away from the stairs and looked at the office door. Panic began to rage through him as he watched the door handle slowly begin to turn. Tom held his breath. Time seemed to stand still as he watched the turning handle, expecting Ms Malignus to walk into her office. He quietly breathed out when the door didn't move but was struck by the realisation of where he was, and what could happen to him if he was caught. There were three quick, sharp taps on the door, then silence. Tom could hear the beating of his racing heart, which felt as though it was about to burst through his chest. Someone was coming. He had to hide... quickly.

He turned back to the stairway and took a breath before stepping inside the cupboard and closing the door behind him.

Ms Malignus walked back into her office and froze the moment she opened the door. Stepping into the room, she closed the door behind her and looked around. She intuitively knew that something was different. Something wasn't right. She closed her eyes and smelt the air with her long nose. *Someone has been here*, she thought to herself. She flicked her tongue out like a lizard and tasted the air. *A child*. She smelled the air again, flicking out her tongue simultaneously. *A boy. A horrible, nasty boy has been here!* Her dark eyes flicked around the room, looking for something unseen. Everything seemed as it should, but she knew it wasn't. Something had changed.

Her senses were on full alert as she prowled slowly to her desk and sat in her large chair, continually scanning the room. She was taking another long inhale, smelling the air, when she heard a quiet creaking sound. In his haste to escape, Tom hadn't closed the cupboard door properly and its old hinges creaked as it gently swung ajar. In a flash, Ms Malignus leapt from the chair and opened the old cupboard doors wide. Standing in front of them, she inhaled again and smiled to herself. She could smell him. She could smell the boy who had been here. She flicked out her tongue and licked her lips before making her way down the stairs, pulling the cupboard doors closed behind her.

The air became colder as Tom made his way down into the darkness. He noticed that the deeper he went the more the steps and walls around him seemed to change, until it was as though he was now walking through a stone passageway rather than the hidden stairs he had first stepped upon. He shivered in the darkness, not knowing whether he was shivering through fear or because of how cold it now was. The musky smell that had been in the office definitely came from this passageway and seemed to grow stronger the further and deeper he went, as the air around him became more foul and more putrid with every step he took. His senses were on overload, screaming against the stench, the darkness and the cold, but he knew he had to keep going. He knew he couldn't stop.

He held his hands out in front of him, unable to see or hear anything, when he suddenly touched something soft. It was right in front of him. He froze, holding his breath. Slowly and reluctantly, he reached his arm out and touched it again. It moved, like a thin veil or curtain, as he pushed against it and as it moved it revealed a faint glow, emanating from somewhere behind it. Tom pushed through and was walking towards the light when he heard a sound… *clack, clack, clack* echoing against the stone walls. Tom moved faster and faster towards the faint light, not wanting the sound and what was making it to catch up with him. The light grew closer and closer. It was coming through a crack in an old rotten wooden door. *Clack, clack, clack.* The footsteps were becoming louder and louder, faster and faster. Ms Malignus was catching him up. Tom pushed open the door and was immediately hit by the most horrid rotting smell. Normally, such a stench would have instantly made him feel sick and he would have vomited there and then, had it not been for the shock of what he saw.

One small, dim light hung from the ceiling of what appeared to be a narrow, dank, dirty cellar. Tom gasped. He could see what looked like rows of children lined up against the stone walls. They were school children, who at first glance appeared to be standing still but when he looked closer he could see that they were all strapped against some sort of wooden frame that was holding them upright. Some of the children had tubes coming from them. Tom couldn't see where the tubes led to or how they were attached to the children, who were lined up in threes and twos, in several rows. In the gloom, Tom couldn't see well enough to count them, but he guessed at maybe ten or eleven. He stood still, open-mouthed, staring at them all. They looked dirty, filthy and rotten, like they had been there for a long time, neglected. Their eyes were all open but they stared lifelessly into the distance. Tom had no idea if they were dead or alive. He moved closer to one of them, trying to see it clearly in the poor light, when he heard it again. *Clack, clack, clack.* The noise brought Tom back to his senses. He began to run through the cellar, trying to ignore the sight of the strapped, motionless children. On the other side of the cellar, he could just about make out some huge bottles and a second rotting door. Thinking quickly, he pushed it open but didn't go through. Instead, he left it open and hid himself behind the rows of children, pushing as far into the shadows of the cellar as he could, trying to make himself as hidden and as invisible as possible. Then in the stench, gloom and darkness he waited, praying that he wouldn't be seen.

Ms Malignus stepped through the rotten door into the cellar. She smiled as she looked at the rows of children and ran her finger over the forehead of the nearest child. There was a small bore hole in the back of the child's neck. Ms Malignus pushed her long, bony finger into it, smiling as she did. She withdrew it and licked the reddish-brown substance that was now covering her finger.

"Little boy," she sang, almost mockingly. "Little boy. Where are you? Come out, come out, little boy."

In his hiding place, Tom shuddered with fear. Through the bodies lined up in front of him, he could just about see the skeletal figure of Ms Malignus, making her way across the space. She crept and stalked her way across the cellar, calling out as she went, constantly looking for any sign of the boy. She scanned the room as she slowly walked through it, her eyes darting everywhere, flicking her tongue, like a lizard, through the air as she went. Then she saw the open door. She snarled and without a second thought ran through it, slamming it shut behind her.

Tom watched her run out of the cellar but stayed hiding where he was, and listened. He wanted to get up and run but didn't move a muscle. *Clack, clack, clack.* The sound slowly disappearing as Ms Malignus made her way to wherever the second door led. Slowly and carefully, Tom stepped out from behind the child he had been hiding behind. It appeared to be a young boy but it was hard to tell as it was so filthy and the room so dark. He looked at the huge bottles. They seemed to contain some sort of sludgy liquid but he didn't want to touch them to find out. Tom could barely breathe and knew he had to get out of the cellar but he was so confused as to where he was and what he was surrounded by that it was difficult to see how he could get out. He staggered quickly in a disorientated haze, passing the children without looking at them, until he reached the door which he had first come through, and which led to the Head's office.

Tom was in shock. He didn't notice the final child he passed. He didn't notice that this one looked cleaner than the others; fresher and newer than the rest. He also didn't notice that this one was wearing red shoes.

18.

Entering the morning assembly, Sophie was beside herself with worry. She prayed that Tom had heard her knocking and had somehow managed to hide in time. Mrs French had seemed disappointed when Sophie had arrived in the hall and re-joined her class but Sophie had barely noticed this, she was so worried about Tom. She sat still in her line as they waited and waited for Ms Malignus to arrive in the hall. She never usually took this long and Sophie had no idea whether her lateness was a good sign or a bad one. When she did eventually arrive, the Head was in even more of a foul mood than she normally was and Sophie hoped her anger meant that Tom had managed to escape.

Ms Malignus swooped into the hall and made her way immediately over to where the teachers were sitting. She whispered something quietly to them. Whatever it was caused them instantly to panic. Miss Betteridge, Mr Dalty and Mrs Atchison stood up and left the hall abruptly whilst the others whispered animatedly between themselves. Whilst the teachers were distracted, Sophie tried to quickly look around for any sign of Tom but he wasn't in the room at all. She caught Lucy's eye. Lucy looked at her in confusion, which quickly turned to fear when she saw how worried Sophie was.

Ms Malignus prowled before the rows of children. Her eyes constantly danced around the room, searching and probing each of the faces in front of her. She didn't say a word but sniffed the air and flicked her tongue in and out, growing more and more agitated and looking increasingly angry with each little flick. The teachers behind her looked fearful. They too seemed agitated and nervous, their attention switching between the children and the headteacher.

The entire hall was silent. Ms Malignus continued to pace, as though she were angrily waiting for something or someone. The only sound the *clack, clack, clack* of her boots as she prowled, the tension growing with each passing minute. All of the children sat completely quiet, many of them with their heads down, not daring to look up for fear of bringing unwanted attention upon themselves. Suddenly, a bang echoed from somewhere outside the hall, breaking the silence. The children jumped in their seats from the noise as Ms Malignus's head snapped in the direction it had come from, a sudden urgency appearing across her face. There was a second, louder bang, accompanied by screams and shouts as Miss Betteridge burst through the hall doors. Sophie noticed a look of shock appear on Mrs French's face. This rapidly vanished and was replaced with one of greed and anticipation, as if her wishes were about to come true. She quickly turned to see Tom being dragged into the room by the muscular PE teacher. He was fighting against her, shouting loudly and trying to escape her grasp, but she was too strong for him and held on to him firmly. He was white as a sheet and looked absolutely terrified.

Ms Malignus remained as still as stone, her eyes locked, staring at the boy as he was dragged towards her whilst the waiting children shuffled nervously in their seats, their hushed whispers fighting to be heard against Tom's shouts and screams of protestation as he continued his vain struggle against the mountainous teacher.

"Shhh," Ms Malignus whispered as he reached her. She placed her long, bony finger on his forehead and he immediately stopped struggling. His eyes remained wide with fear but he stared straight at her, almost frozen under her spell. She sniffed the air around him and her lips curled into a sickening, grotesque smile. "Little boy," she whispered, holding his gaze for a moment before turning him to face the rest of the school. The teachers, sitting up in their seats on the stage, no longer seemed nervous but had become eager and clearly excited at what they were watching.

Sophie stared at Tom. She was close to tears. She looked over to Lucy but she and just about everyone else in the hall was staring at the scene in front of them. Boz was sitting bolt upright in his chair, eyes fixed firmly on Tom, his face a mixture of anger, confusion and worry. Sophie looked at Tom again. He was now staring wide-eyed straight at her. She could feel herself starting to cry.

"This boy!" Ms Malignus shrieked across the hall, contempt and loathing oozing from her voice. "This *child*," she snarled, pulling Tom close to her, "has been creeping in places he should not be in. We know that all children must be in their classes at all times. This is for their education and for their *safety*." She drew out the last word, emphasising each syllable and enjoying the sound and the subdued threat that underlined it.

Mrs French was leaning forward in her seat, licking her lips and grinning intently. "We must not go creeping and skulking in forbidden places," Ms Malignus said, quietly turning to face Tom. His eyes hadn't left Sophie's. Without saying another word, Malignus led him out of the hall. He followed her mechanically, the calmness in his movements betrayed by the manic fear in his eyes. It was almost as if he had no control over his body.

19.

"What the hell is going on, Sophie?" Boz practically shouted in the Den at lunchtime. The rest of the morning had passed in a complete haze for Sophie. She had been present in her lessons but had ghosted through them in a state of numbness and had no idea what any of them were, she was in such shock. Her thoughts and worries were completely taking over any other sense she had. Break time had been cancelled due to the long assembly so this was the first time any of them had had a chance to speak to Sophie about what had happened in the hall.

"I... I... don't know," she stammered back to him.

"What do you mean, you don't know?" he demanded of her angrily. "You must know what happened. This is just like James, all over again. You're supposed to be Tom's friend, aren't you?" Sophie burst into tears.

"Back, off Boz!" Lucy shouted. "Can't you see she's upset?" She put her arms around Sophie to comfort her.

"*She's* upset? Did you see Tom? Did you see what happened?" Boz bellowed angrily. He looked at the two girls furiously. "Tom's done something. What was it, Sophie? What happened?"

"I said back off!" Lucy shouted, pushing Boz in the chest.

"Come on, Luce. Leave it," Jack said, stepping in between them both.

"Hey," Charlie shouted at the two of them. "There's no point any of us fighting, is there? Boz, come with me and calm down." She pulled him away from the others.

"Sit down here, Soph," Jack said, indicating a tree stump and giving her a tissue. "He's only worried, that's all." Lucy was still staring hard at Boz, who was angrily remonstrating with the rest of the group.

"That doesn't give him the right…" She spat the words out.

"I know it doesn't," he calmly replied, "but we can all lose it sometimes, can't we?" Lucy didn't respond but sat down next to Sophie, although she continued to glare at Boz. Sophie wiped her face with the tissue Jack had given her. After a few moments' silence he smiled at her.

"Thanks," she mumbled.

"It's no problem. Are you ok?"

She looked at him blankly. "Did you see Tom's face?" She was overcome by tears.

"I think we all did," Jack replied, his smile now gone. "Do you have any idea what happened?" he quietly asked.

Lucy glared at him but Sophie gave a small nod.

"I saw him," she whispered.

Lucy turned and looked at her. "You saw him?" she asked, shocked. "Doing what?"

Sophie began crying again. "He… he… went into the office," she whispered through the tears.

"What office?" Jack asked.

"Hers," she replied, sniffing. "Malignus's office," she added quietly, barely able to say the name. Jack and Lucy both looked at each other, shocked and concerned.

"What do you mean?" Jack asked carefully.

"What I said," Sophie whispered. "This morning, before assembly, I saw him going in. I tried to get there and stop him but I couldn't. He'd already gone in and then she came. I had to leave him." Sophie began to cry even more.

"That's what she must have meant." Lucy said quietly. Seeing Jack's confused expression, she continued, "When Malignus was talking about creeping in places they shouldn't. She meant him, she was talking about Tom."

Sophie looked up and nodded. She wiped her face with the tissue that Jack had given her; she was crying so much that it had practically disintegrated.

"Here," Jack said, fishing a packet from his pocket, "have a fresh one. Never leave home without clean tissues." He smiled at her, trying to comfort her and lighten her mood a bit.

"It's ok," she replied, sniffing, "I've got one here." She put her hand in her coat pocket to retrieve it but instead pulled out a folded piece of paper.

"What's that?" Jack asked, looking at the note. A small golden key fell from the paper folds. Lucy picked it up and examined it. Sophie unfolded the paper to see what looked like hastily scribbled writing, which was difficult to read.

Sophie, I haven't got much time. I can hear them coming for me. The key is for the old cupboard in Malignus' office. Go there and find them and help them. If they get me then get Boz and the others to help you. Quickly. I'm Sorry. Tom.

Lucy and Jack looked at each other. No one said a word.

Sophie stopped crying and reread the note. "He must have got out and put it in my coat pocket," she whispered, looking up at the key Lucy was holding. "He knew I'd find it."

"Let me read that again," Jack said, taking the note from her and quietly reading it. "Boz," he called, turning to face

Boz and Charlie, who were sitting quietly talking to each other. "Come here, you need to see this."

Boz read the note quietly, whilst the rest of the group watched in silence, the only sound the rustling of the leaves in the trees overhead. He passed the note to Charlie. The tension hung in the air.

"Sophie," Boz said after a few minutes' thought, "tell me exactly what happened and exactly what you saw."

Nobody spoke as Sophie told Boz about all the conversations she'd had with Tom, and about how much he missed the friendship he'd had with him. She told him about how he blamed himself for what had happened with James, and about how much it hurt Tom seeing his friend act so differently every day. She explained that Tom had been determined to find out exactly what was happening in the school, and why all the children seemed to change so much. How distant he'd become and how he hadn't gone to class that morning but that when she had gone to find him, she had seen him entering Malignus's office and couldn't get in after him. She hadn't seen him again until the assembly.

"Why did you go looking for him?" Lucy scolded. "I told you to stay away from him."

"Leave it, Lucy. Not now, eh?" Jack warned. "Well, Boz, what do you think?"

"I think Tom's done what he always does," Boz replied irritably. "He's done something stupid and got himself into trouble. Now, he's trying to drag us in as well. That's what I think."

Everyone in the group remained quiet.

"What, so you're just going to ignore it?" Jack asked flatly.

"Yeah," Boz snapped, "I am and so should you."

Jack looked at him, not believing what he had heard. "No, Boz," he began to argue, "We've ignored this for far too long. Something weird happens here and it's about time we found out what. Tom had obviously had enough of it and went looking for answers. Well, I've had enough, too. Tom did a lot of stupid things but at least he had the guts to try and find out what's going on and to try and put it right, instead of hiding away and pretending it's all ok."

Boz looked up angrily and squared up to him. Ben jumped in between them both.

"I want to help Tom," Sophie said. She stood by Jack and looked at Boz fiercely.

Lucy huffed at her angrily. "Fine. I'm in, too," she said, walking over to Sophie and standing beside her and Jack. "Anyone else?"

Jack looked at Ben. "Sorry mate but Boz is right," Ben said, looking sheepish. "Tom's trouble and always has been. You know that."

"Maybe," Jack replied, "but he was one of us once."

Ben walked away to the other side of the Den and sat down, followed by the rest of the group, leaving just Jack, Lucy and Sophie.

"Right," Jack said, grinning at them. "Let's find out what's going on, shall we?" He turned away and began to walk through the bushes.

"I told you there was a more serious side to him," Lucy whispered to Sophie as they followed him out of the Den.

20.

The three walked quietly through the small woods, back towards the school.

"I'm sorry, guys," Sophie whispered meekly. "I didn't want to cause any problems."

"You haven't," Lucy grumbled. "Tom has. I warned you he was trouble, didn't I?"

Jack, who had been walking just ahead of the girls, stopped and looked at her, a thought crossing his mind. "It's not like that, Lucy," he said, looking at her seriously. "Tom wasn't the problem and he was right, wasn't he? We all know something's going on here don't we? and we've all ignored it for too long. At least Tom tried do something about it. Well, I think it's time we did too." He looked back from where they had come from, towards the Den. "It's a pity not everyone thinks like that, though."

They continued to make their way through the wood silently, and stepped out from behind the large bush onto the field. They looked at the school looming large in front of them. "What's the plan, Jack?" Sophie asked as they walked towards the building.

"I think we should go and see what's in this cupboard in Malignus's office," he answered, not looking at her but staring straight ahead, his focus completely on the school.

"Are you mental?" Lucy snapped, stopping still and looking completely shocked at his suggestion. "We can't go in there. That's what Tom did and he got caught. We don't even know what's happening to him now, do we?"

Jack stopped and turned to look at her, not liking what she was saying.

Sophie linked arms with her. "No, we don't," she said gently, "but we do know that Malignus won't be in there, don't we?"

Lucy looked at her friend disbelievingly. Sophie, who was thinking of Tom and wanted to do whatever it took to help him, smiled and began to walk towards the school again, softly pulling her arm and persuading her to walk with her. "All of the staff lock themselves away in the staffroom at lunchtime, don't they? You even said yourself it's the only time that you can never find any of them."

"It's true," Jack said as they caught him up and the three began walking together across the field. "Even old Thomass goes in there and joins them. She leaves the Watchouts to answer all the phones and look after stuff. I reckon it's probably the only time during the day that the ugly old trout gets off that chair and away from her computer." Sophie laughed and Jack smiled.

"Even Malignus will be in the staffroom," Lucy said, nodding, slowly changing her mind and trying to reassure herself as much as the others. "We'll be ok as long as we keep an eye out, won't we?"

"We will," Sophie answered nervously.

"And as long as we hurry up," Jack said, approaching the school building, "now that we've all agreed, we need to get a move on. We've only got the rest of lunchtime to do this."

They stepped around the corner onto the playground and made their way to the large wooden doors. Lucy looked around to make sure that no one was watching them before they opened the doors and went into the school. To their relief and surprise, the corridors were empty and they managed to successfully make their way to Ms Malignus's office without being seen. Lucy waited at the top of the small alcove to keep an eye out for anyone walking by whilst Jack and Sophie stood outside the door.

"Here goes nothing," Jack whispered, taking a deep breath and smiling at Sophie. He knocked on the door. They both remained absolutely silent and still whilst they waited for a response. The moment seemed to stretch through eternity before Jack breathed out and took hold of the door knob. He closed his eyes and paused to collect his courage before he opened the door and walked through. He breathed a huge sigh of relief when he found the room was empty, and beckoned Sophie and Lucy to follow him in. Lucy closed the door behind her. All three stood and gazed at the ancient oak cupboard in the corner of the room, seemingly entranced by it.

"Quickly… who's got the key?" Jack asked quietly, pulling his senses together and making his way over to it. "I don't want to spend a minute longer in here than we need to."

"Me, I've got it," Lucy replied, reaching into her pocket and pulling out the small golden key. She handed it over to him and without any hesitation he put it straight in the cupboard's lock. As he did so he felt the door slowly push ajar creaking slightly.

"It's not locked," he whispered, even though there was only the three of them in the room. "Let's see what Tom was on about," he said as he opened the doors fully. "What the…?"

His words caught in his mouth as he stared at the flight of stairs leading into darkness. Sophie gasped and, gobsmacked, looked at Lucy. All of them were speechless, completely taken aback. Jack was the first of them to move.

"Come on," he whispered, stepping into the cupboard and onto the stairs.

"Jack, don't … we can't…" Lucy hissed as she watched him slowly descend. Sophie quietly pushed past her and followed him. "Sophie… Jack…" Lucy hissed at them. The quiet stillness of the room and the stairs made her feel as though she were shouting at her friends. She shuddered. "Stop… don't…" she called as loudly as she dared. She watched as the two of them crept down the stairs. Lucy was petrified at the thought of what could be at the bottom but equally as petrified at the thought of remaining in the office alone. She watched as first Jack and then Sophie disappeared in the blackness below. "Sophie," she hissed into the gloom, then, "Jack!" There was no reply.

Lucy looked around the room, realising that she was completely alone. She took a breath and clenched her teeth together. "Fine!" She cursed to herself, taking the key from the cupboard's lock. Stepping inside, she quietly pulled the door closed behind her and began her own flight down the stairs.

Lucy gagged as she stumbled through the dark passageway. The smell coming from the darkness grew stronger with every step that she took. "Sophie," she whispered as loudly as she dared, her voice seeming to bounce off the stone walls and ceiling, echoing all around her. She wanted to run, back the way she had come and far away from this foul-smelling darkness. The last thing she wanted to do was to continue moving forwards but she knew she had to. She had to find the others and reluctantly she pressed on. Deeper and deeper she went into the bowels of the school. She couldn't call out again, even if had she wanted to, due to the fear that was growing inside her. She shuffled forward, listening for any sound that might tell her where Jack and Sophie were, or might even indicate where she was headed.

The passage remained silent and pitch-black but the stench continued to grow. With each passing moment, and with each move forward, she found it more and more difficult to continue. The only sound she could hear was her own stifled breathing and the loud beat of her heart. She kept one hand against the edges of the passage for balance and one out ahead of her, wincing at every unexplained lump or bump she touched, then she felt something soft directly in front of her. It took all of her control not to scream when she made contact with it and she quickly pushed through it, not pausing to wonder what it might have been. She could make out a faint glow up ahead of her and slowly walked towards it, her hand stretched out, then she touched something warm and soft. She froze.

"Sophie?" she whispered quietly, quickly becoming even more afraid. Suddenly, Jack's face appeared in front of her. His eyes were wide with horror and he immediately put his hand up to her mouth, silencing her. He was shaking his head violently, as if he was trying to tell her to stop. As he did so, he raised his finger and put it over his lips, indicating to her to remain absolutely quiet. She nodded in agreement and he moved his hand away. He then pointed behind him and she could make out Sophie's figure, standing against what appeared to be an old door. She had her face pressed up against it. Lucy gently put her hand on Sophie's shoulder. She could feel her shaking underneath her touch. Sophie spun round, startled, and revealed a small thin crack in the door that she had been looking through. She too looked terrified, as though she had seen something horrific. She stepped away from the door, looking as though she was about to be sick.

Now Lucy stepped towards the crack. She could hear strange noises coming from behind it. A mixture of slurping and sucking sounds, combined with soft crunches, and low growls and groans. With increasing trepidation, she slowly leaned forward and looked through the crack.

21.

Lucy felt herself stiffen, her fear increasing sharply. Through the crack in the door she could make out a few shapes amidst the gloom, moving around inside what she thought was a cellar. The tall, thin figure of Ms Malignus came into focus in the dimly lit space. Mrs French and Mr Fields were also there, shuffling about in the dimness. Lucy looked around the cellar and could make out what looked to be several children, lined up in rows along one side. In the middle, Malignus was holding someone by their head. As Lucy's eyes adjusted to the light, she could see that the figure Malignus was holding was Tom. He was strapped to an upright wooden gurney and the lower half of his face covered with some sort of mask. His eyes were wide open and filled with terror. Malignus had one hand over the mask and was holding what looked like a long, thin needle in the other. She was smiling at him and appeared to be whispering something, although Lucy couldn't make out what.

The terror built inside her. Lucy wanted to both run away to safety and to burst inside the cellar to help Tom, in equal measures, but was unable to do either; her fear had her rooted to the spot. She couldn't pull away from the crack in the door and almost yelled out, having to bite her lip to stop herself from making any noise as she watched Malignus push the needle deep into the back of

Tom's neck, the malice in her face visible even in the gloom. He tried to thrash and wriggle away from her but was unable to, due to the restraints. After a brief moment, his struggles stopped and he became still. Lucy could feel the tears welling in her eyes and understood why Jack and Sophie had looked so horrified. She looked at the needle sticking out of the back of Tom's neck. A long, thin tube was attached to the end of it. Lucy's eyes followed the length of the tube, taking her attention away from Tom, and tracked it across to the far side of the cellar, where Mrs French stood. The general gloom meant it was harder for Lucy to see but she was able to make out that the tube was attached to a huge clear bottle that French was holding. The teacher appeared to be struggling to hold the bottle, due to its size, but she didn't drop it. A thick, coppery-red mucous-like liquid began to ooze slowly from the tube into the bottle. Mrs French smiled as she watched it fill.

"Where is the Golem?" Malignus growled, turning to Mr Fields.

"It is coming, Headmistress," the old teacher wheezed. "One more minute."

Lucy looked around the cellar to try and locate Fields, eventually seeing him standing deep in the shadows, in the darkest corner. She couldn't see clearly what he was doing but he seemed to be shaping and moulding something. "The bottle is full, Headmistress, mmm, mmm," Mrs French announced, staggering under its weight as she unhooked the tube.

Malignus looked at her coldly and sneered at how she seemed to be struggling to hold the huge container. "Good," she ran her hand around to the needle at the back of Tom's head, "take it to the staffroom so the others may feed." Mrs French turned and with considerable effort carried the full, heavy bottle through a door on the other side of the cellar, which Lucy hadn't noticed until that moment. A bright light fell upon the room as the door was opened, illuminating the whole area. In that instance, Lucy saw the cellar in full. Rows of children, all strapped to upright wooden pallets, some with tubes similar to the one that was currently hanging from Tom embedded in their necks. They all looked filthy and neglected, and all of them had eyes which were glossed over. The sight nearly made Lucy sick and was gone the moment Mrs French closed the second door.

Ms Malignus slowly withdrew the needle from Tom's neck and licked along the length of it with her tongue. She undid the mask that was strapped to his face and smiled at him. "Little boy," she laughed, looking into his milky-white, glazed over eyes, "Good boy." Tom didn't respond and just hung from his straps. It was as though all his strength and energy had gone.

"The Golem is now ready, Headmistress," Mr Fields called from the corner of the cellar in which he was working. He led a boy out of the shadows. Lucy gasped when she saw who it was, quickly putting her hand over her mouth to stifle the noise.

"Good, it looks perfect," snarled Malignus, walking over to the Golem and looking it over, like someone would look at a new car. "Little mummies and daddies will never know the difference." She turned to Mr Fields, "I shall take it to my office for its instructions. You can go and feed."

Lucy's heart began to race even faster when she heard these words. She turned to Jack and Sophie, fear written all over her face. For a moment, all three held each other's gaze, recognising their own panic mirrored in each other's eyes.

"Quick, she's coming," Lucy whispered as loudly as she dared. Without waiting for any response, she immediately began to make her way back up the passage. Without a sound, the other two followed, all three moving much faster out of the passage than they had gone into it, feeling their way along the walls, moving with urgency but as silently as they could and always listening out for any sound of Malignus following them.

When they reached the first step of the stairs, Lucy clumsily tripped on it. Jack fell on top of her. "Hurry!" Sophie whispered as she speedily helped the others to their feet and they began to climb the steps as quickly but as quietly as possible. Stepping out of the cupboard and back into Malignus's office, Jack made sure to softly close the doors behind him. He gazed longingly at it and ran his hands along the frame, once again enthralled by it and momentarily forgetting the danger they were in. "Jack," Sophie hissed, grabbing him by the arm and forcefully pulling him away. Lucy led them through the office door and into the small alcove. Sophie pulled the door closed and leaned against it. All three stood outside the office and paused for a moment, getting their breath back.

Sophie's eyes were red and her face was pale. "Did you see…?"

"Not here, not now," Lucy said desperately. "Let's get to the yard… to somewhere safe." Jack nodded in agreement and moved in front of the two girls. Lucy took a huge breath, the sick feeling still within her, slowly rising like bile. Without saying another word, Jack looked out from the alcove onto the corridor, to check no one was there. He then slipped around the corner, quickly followed by the two girls. They quietly made their way along the deserted school corridors, outside to the yard, unseen by anyone. When they finally got outside, they huddled in a corner, sucking in as much fresh air as they could. No one spoke or even looked at each other for a while.

Sophie was the first to break the silence. "Did you see that?" she asked, looking directly at Jack. He nodded gravely back at her. "All those children... that was Tom, wasn't it?"

Jack turned to Lucy, ignoring the question. "Lucy, what did you see?" There was an urgency to his voice. She told him about the needles and the huge bottle French had. "I saw that too," he interrupted, "but there was more than one bottle. She was holding one but there were others next to her. They all looked empty, though?"

Lucy shook her head. "No, when Malignus put the needle into his neck it began to fill up with something."

"Poor Tom," Sophie whispered as much to herself as the others, "that's disgusting."

"It was like they were milking him or something," Lucy continued.

"Was he dead?" Sophie asked, doing her best not to burst into tears.

"No, I don't think so," Lucy answered immediately, her answer making her friend breathe out heavily. "I'm sure I saw him move, like he was trying to resist it. That's not all, though. I saw Fields, he was making something in the corner."

"I didn't see him," Jack said. "What was it?"

"I don't know," Lucy replied, "Malignus called it something. What was it?" There was a long silence whilst Lucy tried to recall the information. She didn't really want to think about the horrors in the cellar again. "A Golden, or goal, oh what was it?" She screwed up her face, trying to think. "It sounded something like that, a coalum or something."

"A Golem?" Sophie asked, looking horrified.

"Yeah, that was it. She definitely called it that. A Golem."

"What's one of those?" Jack asked, looking at Sophie.

"A Golem, it's like some sort of monster or puppet," she answered. "It's made from mud or clay and made to look like a person, but in the stories they're always clumsy or brainless lumps."

"Yeah," Lucy interrupted, a sudden realisation showing on her face. "It did look like a person, it looked like Tom, but it wasn't just some lump of clay. It looked exactly like him."

"Maybe it wasn't a Golem, then?" Jack said.

"That's what she said," Lucy insisted. "She called for the Golem and Fields brought Tom out or this Golem thing."

"It doesn't matter what we call it," Sophie interrupted, "all that matters is that Tom and the others are trapped in that cellar."

The school bell rang, to signal the end of lunchtime.

"Don't mention anything to anyone," Jack warned the girls. "Not yet, just pretend that nothing has happened. We'll meet after school outside the school gates. Ok?"

"I can't go to lessons now," Lucy protested, still in shock. "Not after seeing that."

"We have to," Jack argued. "If we don't and we're missing they'll come looking for us. Like they did with Tom." He left his words to hang in the air.

"He's right," Sophie agreed quietly. "We can't give them any reason to think anything has changed, or that we've seen anything. Please, Lucy, you have to go in."

Lucy stared at them both and realised that they were right. Reluctantly, she agreed to go into her lessons as normal and meet them after school. "Stay safe," she whispered to Sophie, hugging her before leaving to join Jack in their line.

Sophie stood behind Penelope. She looked at the girl in a whole new way and wondered if she was actually

Penelope at all, and not one of those Golem things. Could the real Penelope be tied up in that horrible cellar as well? She looked over to where Jack stood. He was staring at the floor, his shoulders slumped as though he was carrying some great weight. The cheeky smile and twinkle in his eye had been replaced with a look of seriousness and worry. Lucy was standing close to him in their class line, still looking as though she were in shock. As Sophie's class began to enter the building, she wondered how she now looked, feeling a twinge of jealousy that they at least had each other for support, whilst she was left on her own.

22.

Ms Malignus was furious. How could a child have entered her cellar? How could a child have known of their secret? She shuddered at the thought of what could have happened; what might have been, had they not caught him. She paced her office, prowling like an animal stalking its prey, contemplating what had happened that day. "What if he wasn't alone?" she whispered to herself. "What if there were others?"

She had smelled something different in the passage, perhaps noticed another smell; a child's smell. It was difficult to tell because of all the other scents rising from the cellar. She had believed the child she had now caught was acting alone but what if she had been wrong? What if there had been more?

A knock on her office door pulled her away from her thoughts. "What?" she shrieked. The door slowly opened and Mr Parkes meekly peered in.

"It is time, Headmistress," he said quietly, never once looking up at her. She flew across the room to him and grabbed him by his beard, swinging him violently into her office. He landed heavily and remained crumpled in a heap on the floor.

"Time!" she yelled at him. "It is only time when I say it is time." She shrieked in rage. "What if I were to drain you? What if I were to feed you to them?" Mr Parkes remained silent and motionless on the floor. Ms Malignus stepped over his cowed body and returned to sit at her desk, taking long, deep breaths. She looked at the pathetic teacher lying curled up on the floor and laughed at him. "You are more hair than food. No one would want to eat you," she mocked, looking away from him in disgust. "You are pathetic. Get up."

It was then that she happened to notice that the small, thin secret drawer in her desk was slightly open. A strange feeling of anxiety and fear began to rise within her. She opened the drawer and swallowed hard. The key was missing!

"Get out!" she screamed at Mr Parkes. "It is gone. Get out." He scrambled to his feet and tried to run out of the door before she could get to him. She leapt over the desk and slammed the door shut behind him, still screaming at him to get out.

"How could it be gone?" she asked herself, angrily pacing the room. "It can't be gone. No one else knows of it. It must be here." She began to search the office, panicking and pulling drawers from her desk, tipping the contents onto the floor and looking wildly around the room. She stopped and looked at the ancient cupboard. *The boy*, she thought, *he must have it. It must be with him.* She flew through the unlocked cupboard and down the passageway to the cellar as fast as she could, straight to Tom.

She stood in front of him, glaring angrily. He appeared totally lifeless but she knew that he wasn't. She knew that he was still very much alive but in a state of sleep. "Where is it, little boy?" she growled at him, searching his pockets with her long, bony fingers. "Where have you put it?" She froze when she couldn't find it and stared into his milky eyes. "There are others?" she whispered to him, "There must be others, who have you given it to?" She could feel her anger rising up but also a sense of unease. She hated unknowns and the possible threats they might bring to her. She began to breathe slowly, calming herself. She had to make sure no one found out about the real reason for the school. This boy, along with whomever he had given her key to, had now threatened that secret. She thought of the teachers, up above, waiting in her school, waiting for their Sanguine, their reward. She detested them and their animal natures. She knew she was better than them, a higher caste than all of them, but she also knew she needed them to herd the children and maintain the façade of an educational establishment. It was her role to milk the children and, along with the other schools in the academy, to provide the directors and her kind with the Sanguine they needed to live. The teachers were base animals but were an essential part of this operation. Could she use them to eliminate this threat?

She stroked Tom's cheek. "Who are your friends, little boy?" she whispered to him, looking around the cellar at all of the children, all restrained and silently lifeless, before turning back to Tom. She leaned in close, her face practically touching his. "I will find them," she whispered quietly, with malice. "Oh yes, I will find them, and then we will feed from them. They will join you and we will feed."

23.

Tom, or what was now being passed off as Tom, was absent from all of his lessons that day and in spite of her fears and worries or the fact that she wanted to get as far away from the place as possible, Sophie did exactly what they had agreed to do, making sure that she remained inconspicuous in the class and doing her best not to draw any attention to herself. She didn't really pay any attention to the lessons, though, and found it impossible to concentrate on anything other than the hidden cellar and all of the children within it, including Tom. She thought in horror about what Lucy had seen and what she said had happened. Sophie wondered what exactly she meant, and what exactly was happening to them. She was disgusted that such a place could exist and that the teachers and Malignus were part of it. What sort of person could do the things they were doing and how on earth could they get away with treating the children in such a way? She shuddered, thinking about the Golems. Surely the parents would notice that their own children had been replaced? She thought of her own home. Would her parents notice? Her dad was always at work and when her mom wasn't working she was still always busy. Her mom didn't even give her lifts to and from school anymore, now that she was supposedly more settled. Sophie realised that she spent most of her time shut in her bedroom, listening to music and talking to her friends on the phone. She felt guilty when she recognised that, given the amount of time she actually spent with her parents, maybe they wouldn't notice if she was replaced as well.

After school, she quickly made her way to the gates to wait for Lucy and Jack. The afternoon had seemed to take forever to end and she had a headache from all of the thoughts that had been running around her brain. Whilst she was waiting, she saw a boy walking down the drive towards her. "Tom!" she called out, in that moment forgetting everything that had happened. She beamed at him; she had been worrying about him so much that she could barely contain her happiness and excitement to see him.

However, he looked straight ahead into the distance with a glazed look on his face, not seeming to recognise or even register she was there. "Tom," she called again, knowing it was useless. He continued to ignore her and walked straight past, through the gates. She quietly watched him walk away, tears coming easily to her eyes again.

"He's gone, hasn't he? Been replaced?" asked a voice behind her. Sophie turned to see Lucy standing motionless by the gate. She had watched Tom ignore Sophie. She could see how upset Sophie was.

"Yeah, I think he has," Sophie answered, wiping away the tears. "Where's Jack?"

"I'm here," he answered as he walked through the gates. He looked at Sophie and could see she had been crying. Lucy discretely shook her head, telling him not to ask any questions.

"Any ideas what we're going to do?" Sophie asked bluntly, wanting to take her attention away from Tom. She was desperate for them to do something; anything that could help him and the others.

Jack shook his head. "Nothing here," he answered, looking around. "There's too many eyes and ears here and we don't know who we can trust. Can you both come to mine tonight?" The girls both nodded. "Good, we'll do that, then. Meet at mine and we'll think of something there."

"I'll come round to yours and walk down with you," Lucy said to Sophie, not giving her the option to say no.

"Ok," Jack continued. "My mom goes out to work at half past seven. Get to mine for around about then and don't say anything to anyone. Not yet, ok?" The girls nodded their agreement and Jack smiled at them. "See you later, then." He paused for a moment, not really wanting to leave them, before he slowly started walking away. He looked at the ground as he walked and very quickly became lost in his thoughts. The two girls watched him walk off into the distance.

"It'll be ok, won't it?" Sophie asked Lucy, desperately looking for any solace.

"It has to be," Lucy quietly answered.

24.

*I*t was quite a pleasant spring evening as Lucy and Sophie walked slowly together to Jack's house. The birds were singing and a gentle breeze blew through the trees.

A silence hung between the two of them as they walked along the pavement, both lost in their own thoughts. Lucy slipped her arm into Sophie's. They were both glad to have the other supporting them.

"Did you see how many children were there?" Sophie asked, continuing her thoughts. "And that smell. It reeked. How can any of this be happening? How can it be real?" Lucy didn't answer but carried on walking in silence. She didn't want to think about any of it let alone try to find answers. Sophie didn't push the conversation any further, even though the questions didn't stop spinning round her mind.

They walked the rest of the journey in silence, until they arrived at Jack's house. Lucy knocked on the door and he quickly answered. He had been waiting impatiently for them. "Come in," he said without any preamble. They followed him into the house. Jack lived alone with his mom, who was now at work, and although the house appeared to be completely empty, the three went up to his bedroom and he shut the door. It was a decent-sized room, with a bed against the wall. There was a small desk with a chair tucked underneath it; the type you might find in an office, and he'd obviously tidied up for their visit. Lucy threw herself onto his bed whilst Sophie sat in the chair. "I've been thinking," he said, sitting on the bed and leaning against the wall, "the only way we can actually know what's going on down those stairs is if we go back and have a proper look." He looked at Sophie first before turning to Lucy.

"We can't do that," Lucy sat up sharply. "We'll definitely get caught if we do that. We were lucky today and we can't bank on getting lucky again."

Jack stopped her. "No, you're right, we can't," he agreed, nodding his head enthusiastically, "not if we go when there are teachers there, but what if we go when there aren't any?"

Lucy looked at him, confused. "What do you mean?"

Sophie's eyes widened with shock as she realised what he was suggesting. "You want to break into the school?" she asked, answering Lucy's question for him. "When there's no one else around?"

Jack nodded and grinned at them.

"Are you mad?" Lucy snapped furiously, "How are we going to get in? What happens if we get caught?"

"Well, we can't just sit here and do nothing, can we?" Jack argued back. A heavy silence fell between the two of them. Lucy slumped back on the bed, her arms folded, shaking her head and muttering under her breath.

"I agree with Jack," Sophie said eventually, breaking the tension but avoiding Lucy's glare and facing Jack. "We need more information; as much as we can get, before we tell anyone. This is the only way we can do it."

"And how do you propose we do this?" Lucy asked forcefully, clearly not impressed.

"I've thought about that," Jack replied. "We can leave a window open before we leave school and use it to get in." Lucy rolled her eyes at him. "We only have to get in when there's no one there," he continued, "We've already got the key to that cupboard, haven't we?" He waited for a response but when none came added defiantly, "It's the only way, Lucy."

Lucy stared at her friends, not believing what they were saying. They both sat silently, looking firm and resolute. This was the only option available to them. "What if you're wrong, though? What if this isn't the only way?" she asked.

Jack shrugged his shoulders, "Sometimes it's better to act and be wrong than to do nothing at all."

Lucy huffed at him and shook her head. No one spoke. Eventually, after weighing up their arguments, Lucy sighed, "I can't believe I'm saying this but I suppose we're in trouble whatever we decide, aren't we? Whether we act or not?"

Jack smiled at her. "You're right," he said, courage and conviction growing within him. "If we do nothing, we take the risk that eventually they'll get us and turn us into one of those Golem things. I'd rather go down fighting and get caught actually trying to do something to stop them."

"When are we doing it, then?" Sophie asked.

"I reckon we do it tomorrow night," Jack replied quickly.

Nobody spoke, each of them thinking through the consequence of the decision they were making.

"Ok," Lucy agreed. "We'll do it tomorrow. Sophie, you can tell your mom you're staying at mine. I'll tell mine I'm staying at yours… in case we're out late!" she added dryly.

Sophie agreed. "What are you going to say, Jack?"

"I'll think of something," he replied, "My mom is on nights so as long as we're done before she gets back I'll be fine."

They spent the rest of the evening planning what they were going to do the next day. As the girls were leaving, Jack hugged them both. "We'll be fine. We're doing the right thing."

"Let's hope so," Lucy said as she walked out of the door. Jack's smile disappeared as he closed the door behind them. He looked at his empty house and wondered if his mom would notice if he was caught and replaced by a Golem.

25.

The sun was shining and there wasn't a cloud in the sky. Jack was at the school early, waiting by the gates for Sophie and Lucy to arrive. Sophie was first. She saw him waiting, leaning against the wall, and as she approached noticed how exhausted he looked, like he hadn't slept much. He gave her a tired smile when he saw her.

"No sign of Lucy yet?" she asked. "Are we still going to do this?"

"No there isn't, and yes I hope so," he answered. "We've got to do this, Sophie. I've thought about nothing else all night."

"No, neither have I," she agreed, looking at him positively. "I can't see anything else we can do, either." A long pause hung between the two of them as they thought about the possible ramifications of what they were agreeing to. They looked at each other without speaking.

Jack took a nervous breath. "Sophie, I think we need to tell the others," he said tentatively.

"Are you sure? Boz wasn't exactly keen to listen last time we spoke!"

"I know," Jack answered, "but we didn't know anything then, did we?"

"We don't know a fat lot now, Jack," she replied angrily. She was still upset at the way Boz had cast Tom away and refused to help them.

"But we do know something, don't we?" he said quickly. "Yesterday, we only knew about Tom, and Boz has got his issues with Tom, but now we know more, don't we?"

Sophie didn't answer him, instead staring down the long driveway towards the imposing school.

Jack continued, "Once Boz hears about what we saw, he can't just sit back and do nothing, can he?"

"Can't he?" she snapped, turning to face him.

Jack didn't respond and for a moment the two of them stood facing each other, waiting to see who would speak first. Eventually, Jack turned away from her and looked down the road. "Here's Lucy now," he said, without turning back.

Sophie noticed how, like Jack, Lucy looked pale and tired, as though she too hadn't had much sleep.

"Are we still doing this, then?" Lucy asked as she drew close enough to speak, echoing Sophie's original question and without any form of greeting. Jack and Sophie both answered together that they were.

"But," Jack continued, making sure to get his side of the argument in first, "I think that we ought to tell the others. Sophie isn't too sure about that, though," he added, looking at her. By now, children were starting to walk past them, through the gates and onto the drive. Boz walked past, eyeing the three of them curiously, and gave a half nod of acknowledgement before continuing down the drive.

"I can see why she'd think that," Lucy said as she watched Boz walking away, "but I can honestly say that I think it's the best idea you've had since any of this started,

Jack. I agree, they should know what's going on, or else what are we doing any of this for?"

"That's settled, then," Jack said, pleased that she was siding with him, and turning away from Sophie, who looked as though she was about to argue back. "We'll meet in the Den and then we'll tell the others."

By now, more and more children were turning up for school. Some were being dropped off by parents and others were walking. The area by the gates was becoming much busier and more than a few children looked at the trio as they walked past.

Sophie was beginning to feel self-conscious. "We'd best go," she said, reluctant to leave her friends. "I'll see you both later." She turned away from them and walked through the gates.

Jack watched her walk away then turned to Lucy. "I'd hate to be going in there alone," he said, "at least there's a few of us together. She's got no one now."

"She's got us," Lucy objected forcefully, "and she knows she has."

Jack sighed and gave a small nod of agreement. "Yeah, she has," he said.

They watched Sophie become lost amongst the other children on the yard.

"Come on. Let's go," Lucy said.

They made their way through the gates, aware that the day ahead was fraught with danger.

That morning, Sophie tried to concentrate as best as she could and gave her teachers no reason to notice or even look at her within the class. Try as she might, however, she couldn't stop her thoughts returning to Tom. The real Tom, stuck in that cellar below Ms Malignus's office, with all of the other children. She looked at his Golem and couldn't believe how much it looked like him. She had wondered how his parents, how any of the parents, couldn't notice that they weren't actually their real children, but now seeing this thing, this imposter so close up, she could see how it could easily pass itself off as Tom. It was sitting in his seat, doing his work and wearing his clothes. The only difference she could make out between them was the small orange badge that it wore. She had an idea.

As soon as morning break arrived, she went looking for Lucy and Jack. "Badges!" she blurted out.

Jack looked at her, confused.

"What?" Lucy asked, equally unsure.

"That's how we can do it," Sophie continued, barely noticing their puzzled looks. "That's how we can get around school without anyone suspecting or stopping us... badges!" She looked eagerly at them.

"I'm still not with you, Sophie," Jack said, still looking confused.

A realisation slowly began to dawn upon Lucy, however. She smacked him in the arm. "The orange badges, Jack."

"That's it," Sophie said enthusiastically. "All of them, all of the Golems, wear the orange prefect badges. If we can get some then we won't have to sneak around school. We'll be able to come and go as we please, won't we?" She smiled at Jack expectantly.

"Ok?" he replied, still not as enthusiastic as the others, "but where do we get them from?"

Sophie's face fell at the spanner he had just thrown into her plan.

"The library," Lucy said, quick as a flash. "I've seen them there. Harper keeps a box of them on her desk."

"Harper?" asked Sophie. "She's the librarian?"

"Yeah."

"I've seen them, too," Sophie replied, beginning to grow excited again. "It's as you said, they're there in a box, right on her desk."

Jack looked at the two grinning girls. "Ok," he conceded. "It might work."

"Might?" Lucy said, hitting him again. "Jack, it's a great idea. Well done, Sophie."

"Yeah, it is," he replied, rubbing his arm and smiling at Sophie. "Well done, Soph."

She grinned back at the two of them.

"We can't go to the library together," Jack said to Lucy, "there's no way Dalty is going to let the two of us leave his lesson, but if you two can both try and get out at the same time, one of you can distract Harper whilst the other one gets the badges." He looked at Sophie, "What have you got next?"

"P.E., with Betteridge."

"Ok, well if you two can do this," he replied, "then we can take Boz to that cellar rather than just tell him about it."

During the next lesson, Jack watched as Lucy approached Mr Dalty. His room was impossibly hot and his sweat patches had soaked most of his shirt. Jack felt disgusted looking at the sweaty teacher and grew nervous as he watched Lucy talking to him. He had no idea what she was saying but noticed the man's grin grow wider.

Jack let out a sigh of relief and silently wished her luck as she walked out of the room.

Sophie was already outside the library, waiting nervously for Lucy just where she couldn't be seen from inside the room.

"How long have you been waiting?" Lucy asked quietly when she arrived.

"Not long," Sophie replied, "I told Betteridge that I'd twisted my ankle and she sent me back to the changing room."

Lucy chuckled. "I used your trick and told Dalty I had a water infection," she grinned. "You should have seen how the creep smiled at me when I said it," she added, shuddering.

Sophie looked at her nervously. "What if we get caught?"

"Don't worry," Lucy replied. "Harper is one of the better ones. All she cares about is her precious books. Besides, this library is huge, she'll never know. I'll get her away from the desk, you come in and grab the badges. Easy." She smiled, trying to relax her friend, who just nodded back at her.

As agreed, Lucy went into the library first, whilst Sophie waited outside. She counted quietly in her head before entering, just in time to see the backs of both Lucy and Mrs Harper as they walked away. Moving as quickly and as quietly as she could, Sophie approached the desk. It looked no different to the last time she had seen it and the box was exactly where she was expecting it to be. She quickly grabbed a handful of the small orange badges and put them in her pocket before silently walking out of the room. Her heart was pounding and her thoughts racing wildly. She couldn't believe how easy that was but she couldn't risk waiting for Lucy and quickly returned to the girls' changing room to wait for the end of the lesson.

Jack watched as Lucy walked back into the sweltering classroom. She made eye contact with him and gave a quick shrug of her shoulders. Jack's eyes widened. What did that mean? Lucy looked away and he quickly looked back down at his work, his mind racing. The rest of the lesson seemed to drag on. For every minute that passed, all Jack could think about was whether they had been successful or not and, if not, what would be happening to Sophie? As soon as the lesson had finished and they were safely out of the room, he approached Lucy.

"Well?" he hissed as they walked in single file along the corridors. "How did it go?"

"I don't know," Lucy whispered back. "Sophie was gone when I came out of the library. I don't know what happened to her."

"Talking is not permitted in the corridors," boomed a voice from somewhere close to them. Jack bit his tongue and looked forward. He wanted to know what had happened but knew he would have to wait until they got to the Den.

26.

Sophie was already waiting for Jack and Lucy by the corner of the school building by the time they managed to get outside.

"Sophie!" Lucy called excitedly when she saw her, "where did you go? I've been worried sick about you." She threw her arms around her friend.

"I'm sorry, Lucy," Sophie replied, "I wanted to wait but I couldn't risk hanging about the corridors. I went back to the changing rooms. Betteridge hadn't even realised I had left them."

"Never mind that," Jack said urgently. "How did you get on?"

Sophie smiled at them both and pulled a handful of badges from her pocket.

"Sophie, that's brilliant!" Lucy cried excitedly.

Jack nodded his approval. "Well done, Sophie." He looked thoughtful, perhaps readying himself for the inevitable confrontation with Boz. "Come on, let's go and find the others."

When they arrived at the Den they were surprised to see that Ben was alone. He was sitting eating his lunch and smiled at them as they entered the clearing.

"Alright, guys," he said, "I'm glad you're here. I thought I was going to be spending lunch on my own." He laughed.

"Alright, Ben," Jack replied, looking around the Den. "Where is everyone? We need to speak to you all urgently."

Ben looked at Jack warily. "We're not going to have any more bother are we, mate?"

"That was Boz, not me," Jack replied defensively.

"I'm just saying," Ben answered, sighing, "we're all meant to be mates, aren't we?"

Kate and Harry appeared through the bushes. When they saw Lucy they both gave her a big hug.

"It's strange on the yard today," Harry said. "There's a real tension in the air."

Growing impatient, Jack huffed at them.

"What's up, Jack?" Ben asked, starting to get concerned.

"I need you all here," Jack snapped. "Where are the others?"

Ben gave Lucy and Sophie a curious look but they both turned away. He checked the group, seeing who was there. Boz, Claire and Charlie hadn't arrived yet.

Ben looked at his watch then at Jack, who seemed very anxious and on edge. "It's a bit weird, they're normally here by now." Sophie and Lucy also seemed to be tense and nervous. It was as if the three of them were waiting for something to happen. "What's going on, mate?" Ben asked Jack again, getting up and walking over to him but before he could answer, Claire and Charlie came crashing into the Den. Both looked upset and afraid. Claire was crying.

"It's Boz," she blurted out through her tears. "She's got Boz."

They all gathered around the two girls. Kate and Harry sat Claire down and began to try and console her.

"What do you mean, *she*? What's happened to Boz?" Lucy asked quietly, not really wanting to know the answer.

"Malignus… was on the… yard," Charlie stuttered.

"What, now?" Ben asked, shocked at the news.

"Yeah," Charlie replied, "she was ahead of us in the line as we went outside. We followed out after her but Boz was already outside and he didn't see her." She looked at Claire, who was still crying and being comforted by Harry and Kate. "She must have seen him as he walked around the building. I've never seen anyone move so fast. We waited on the yard. Then we saw her, dragging him back onto the yard and into the school. He was trying to free himself but she was so strong. He just couldn't escape. We had to wait until we knew she had gone before we came here."

"What was she doing on the yard?" Ben asked, shocked to hear the news. "There's never any teachers on the yard at lunch."

"It's because of Tom," Sophie whispered. Lucy looked at her, eyes wide with fear. "She knows that he saw them, remember she said in the assembly that he'd been creeping in places. She's on about the cellar, he saw them and that's why they were all looking for him."

"What cellar?" asked Ben, but nobody answered him.

"So she's checking," Jack said, as though talking to himself. "She's checking the yard to see if anyone else is sneaking off anywhere, she's checking to see who knows what. When she saw Boz go around the corner, she grabbed him."

"We need to be really careful, Jack," Lucy whispered quietly.

"We've got to help him," Sophie said quickly, "before she turns him into one."

"It'll be too late now," Jack replied solemnly.

"What are you three going on about?" Ben demanded.

Jack took a breath. "There's a secret in this school. A horrible, foul, evil one, and we've found out what it is. There's a secret cellar. It's under the school."

"What?" Ben asked, not believing what he was hearing.

"It's true, Ben," Lucy said. "There's a secret door in Malignus's office which leads to it." She could see the anger beginning to rise in him.

"Rubbish!"

"Listen to them!" Sophie shouted, jumping up and looking him straight in the face. All of the group were now focused on her. Claire had stopped crying and a strange hush fell over them. The silence hung in the air. No birds could be heard singing and even the trees had seemed to stop swaying in the breeze.

"She takes them there and does things to them," Lucy continued as a look of fear crept over her face and her voice began to waver. "I saw her put a needle into Tom's neck. He was tied up and couldn't move, it was like she was draining or milking him, and Fields was there, making something... making a..." She paused, unsure of the word, and looked to Sophie for help.

"A Golem!"

"Yeah, Golems," Lucy continued, "they look like the kids, she replaces the real kids with these Golems and they do everything the kids would." She looked at Ben and then at the girls.

"That's why they all become different and act strangely," said Jack, "James, Tom, all of them. They've been swapped with these Golems. The real ones are locked in this cellar. The same thing is going to happen to Boz."

The spring sunshine struggled to penetrate the den and the shadows seemed to close in around them.

"I'm not listening to this rubbish," Ben snarled, breaking the tension that had grown. He shook his head and turned away.

"It's true!" Lucy shouted.

"No, it's not," he shouted back. "It's all rubbish! I don't know why you're all saying it but listen to yourselves. It's all rubbish!" He turned to Claire, Harry, Charlie and Kate. "Come on, let's go. Leave this lot to their Golems." The girls helped Claire back to her feet.

Claire looked at Lucy, "You shouldn't make up horrible stories like that." She sniffed through her tears, which had started falling again. They began to walk through the clearing.

"Ben," Jack called to his friend's retreating back, "It's all true. We're breaking into the school tonight to save them and to try and stop all of this."

Ben turned back, as if he was going to say something, but didn't. The two boys just stared at each other angrily, neither wanting to be the one to back down, before Ben eventually tutted and turned away, following the girls through the clearing and leaving Jack, Sophie and Lucy alone.

27.

Ben sat in class and looked over to where Boz was sitting, quietly getting on with his work. The argument he'd had at lunchtime with Jack, Sophie and Lucy was still playing on his mind, which meant he was finding it hard to concentrate on anything else. It was less than an hour ago that Malignus had taken Boz; how could anything have possibly happened to him in such a short space of time? He seemed the same to him, certainly to look at, at least. How could he have been replaced with anything, one of these Golem things, and no one have noticed? The idea was ridiculous. Ben shook his head and got back on with his work, silently telling himself off for being stupid.

At the end of the lesson, he made sure that he was behind Boz when they lined up. "Oy, Boz," he whispered quietly as they walked down the corridor towards their last lesson. "Boz, what happened with Malignus at lunchtime?" Boz carried on walking. *He can't have heard me,* Ben thought. "Oy, Boz," he repeated as loudly as he dared.

Boz stopped walking and turned around to face him. "Talking is not permitted in the corridors," he said mechanically before turning back around and continuing to class.

Ben was stunned to hear these words coming from his friend. He was even more shocked to see the small orange badge that was pinned to Boz's school uniform. In a trance, he continued to his next lesson, mind racing with possible explanations for Boz's strange manner.

As they sat in their seats for the next lesson, Ben continued to be distracted. He was still thinking about everything that had been said in the Den and still trying to come up with plausible reasons for Boz's strange behaviour when he was pulled from his thoughts by Mrs French's voice calling across the classroom.

"Barry," she called, a greedy smile spread across her face. Ben watched as Boz looked up. "Come and hand these letters out mmm, mmm."

Boz calmly stood up and walked over to her desk to collect the letters, which he then began to hand out, his face completely blank and emotionless. Now Ben knew something was different. Mrs French had never asked Boz to do a job. She only ever asked prefects to do things in the class and Boz hated being called Barry; he always pulled a face at the sound of his real name but he gave no reaction to French calling him it. Ben watched as Boz made his way around the room, handing out the letters. As he approached Ben's desk, Ben studied his face closely. Boz made no eye contact and moved away, as if he had never seen him before. Ben's stomach lurched and he felt sick. Suddenly, Jack's notion didn't seem so ridiculous. Could the things he, Lucy and Sophie had said be true?

After school, he made his way as quickly as he could to the gates. He wanted to catch Boz and Jack before they left.

"Boz," he called out as his friend walked past him. "Boz." There was no reply or any sign of recognition; Boz simply walked straight on, without once looking back. Ben couldn't believe that his friend would ignore him like that. The spring sun was shining but Ben felt cold inside. Something had to be wrong.

"Told you, mate," came a voice from behind. Ben turned to see that Jack was leaning against the school wall. He had a grim look on his face and was watching Boz walk away. "It's funny, Sophie said Tom was out of class all day when they caught him. She must have taken her time with him."

Ben looked at him resolutely. "All those things you said, they can't be true? It wouldn't be allowed, it's awful."

"It wouldn't be allowed?" Jack mocked, turning his attention from Boz and staring at Ben. "Who'd believe it? You didn't!" He paused to let his words sink in. "I know it's awful, mate. That's why we're going to stop it."

Ben turned silently and watched as Boz walked away. "You're saying that that isn't really Boz, that he's actually still in school? Right now?" Jack quietly nodded. "And there are others, down there in that cellar with him?" Again, Jack nodded. "I can't get my head around this," Ben said wheeling around to look at him.

"It's true, Ben. All of it," Jack said, a cold, steely look upon his face. "I've seen it."

"You're right that no one would believe any of this, Jack," Ben replied quietly.

"Which is why it's up to us," Jack responded. Ben remained quiet.

"We're meeting here at nine tonight," Jack continued. "If you want to do something, you can meet us. If not, then keep your mouth shut and keep pretending it's not happening." He began to walk away.

"Jack," Ben called out after him. Jack turned back around. "I'm sorry, mate."

Jack smiled ruefully. "So am I," he said, walking away.

28.

*M*s Malignus stood in the dark cellar and looked at the rows of motionless children lined up, strapped to their gurneys before her. Various tubes and wires connected them, keeping them alive. Though she hated them, she knew how precious they were. It was their thoughts, their innocence, their very youthfulness, which created the Sanguine that she and her race needed to exist.

She thought of their history; a matriarchal society hiding in the shadows throughout the ages, made up of castes who had their place and value. 'Bellualis', they called themselves, although they had been named many things over the centuries: Mormo, Lamia, vampyre, witch, and many stories and myths had been made about them, often instigated and perpetuated as a form of propaganda by those in the Clerical caste, such as Mrs Harper, who quietly influenced and manipulated society's principles and values in order to maintain their secrecy. Some of the stories were truer than others but all of them shared a common theme. The Sanguine. This was their truth, they needed the precious Sanguine to survive and it was her responsibility to milk it from the children in her charge. Over the centuries they had evolved; their methods had changed, becoming more and more sophisticated, slowly infiltrating the structures of society: police, educational establishments and the like. Gone were the days of violence and gore. Now, they were everywhere; hospitals, orphanages and schools were used to harvest the children and replace them with the Golems created from the earth by the likes of Mr Fields and others in the Elder caste. Methods of making them were advanced now, and far superior to the crude attempts made long ago. The Golems they now created were perfect, to the smallest detail. What better way of maintaining Sanguine crops than keeping a supply of children, able to be milked regularly, at hand? And when they grew of an age to leave school, it was a simple matter of allowing them to replace their Golem and live their lives as normal. Obviously with no memory of their captivation or milking.

Parents, she thought to herself with contempt, did not know their children to begin with and any 'peculiar' or 'odd' behaviour was simply put down to 'hormones' and 'teenage years'. She smiled at the simplicity of the whole operation. Of course, there were those amongst her brethren who still longed for the ancient ways of blood gathering and death but she was not one of them. She recognised the importance of having a hierarchy and cultivating their feed to ensure the survival of their species. It was she who was stronger, faster and more intelligent, who could master and control the more animalistic members of her race, such as the teachers in her school. And it would be she who would surpass the directors who monitored and imposed their command, and take her rightful place on the high council, assuming full authority and power.

She thought of the teachers in the school and their base animal natures. She knew that entrance to the cellar could only be gained via the passageway in her office. If they were able to freely enter, they would destroy the harvest and ruin their Sanguine crops in their lust and desire. She hated having to rely upon their restraint but was wise enough to know that they had their role to play. However, mistakes had been made which could lead to devastation if they were allowed to bear fruit. Only she could permit entry to the cellar but this had now been broken. She looked at Tom and Boz, both stored next to each other. This one had broken the control she'd had. He had taken her key; the only key which could control the entrance to the passage, an entrance which was now open, unlocked and vulnerable. She had him and she had found his friend but still her key was missing. *There are others who may come*, she thought. Others who might enter the cellar and she must now be ready for them.

She turned away from the children and walked to the door at the far side of the cellar, which led to the staffroom. She stepped through the doorway. Immediately to her left there was a large alcove. It was full of huge glass bottles, lined up on a straining shelf. Each bottle was full with a thick, copper-red liquid. She took one down from the shelf and smiled. She was so much stronger than the others, who often seemed to struggle lifting such a weight. She carried it up to the passageway, stopping at a wooden door that could only be opened from inside the passage. She listened at the door to the grunts and wheezing coming from the staff in the staffroom on the other side. *Animals*, she thought with disdain. She opened the door and entered the room.

"It is time," she announced to the teachers, who had been waiting for their reward, each of them holding a small goblet, ready to receive their feed. She watched as their greedy eyes gazed at the bottle in her hands. She waited, looking at them imperiously, knowing that she was better than them. After a moment, the room became deathly silent.

"You have been lazy," she snarled at them. "You have been neglectful of your duties." She swished the liquid in the bottle and watched as Mrs French's tongue flicked in and out of her mouth as she anticipated her feed. Mr Dalty grinned stupidly at her whilst other teachers fidgeted and became agitated in their eagerness for the Sanguine. Only Mrs Harper and Mr Fields remained calm, passive and unmoved. She looked at them. *That is because they are different*, she thought. Their castes and their roles elevated them above the others, but not above her.

"You have allowed children to roam unobserved," she snarled at her staff. "You have not known where they are." Several of the teachers began to look fearful as the threat in her voice increased. "You!" she spat at Mrs French. "A boy from your class was caught out of lessons." Mrs French squirmed. Ms Malignus turned to Mr Dalty, "And you, you have also allowed children to leave your class unescorted." Both teachers stared at the floor, avoiding her gaze. Mr Dalty was no longer grinning. "This is not acceptable!"

There was now total silence in the room. All of the teachers were passive and still. "We must ensure the safety of the harvest. We must ensure that the school is safe and secure. At all times!" She could see the staff physically begin to tense and smiled to herself, relishing the power and control she had. "There will be no feeding until I am satisfied the school is once again under proper control. You will patrol the corridors, you will patrol the school, and you will patrol the grounds at all times, day and night, until I am happy. Am I understood?" There was no response. "Am I understood?" She growled dangerously.

"Yes, Headmistress," came a mumbled reply.

Ms Malignus glared at the staff for a moment before turning to Mrs Harper. "Helena, as record keeper and cleric, you may feed. It is your responsibility to ensure that these patrols are done." Mrs Harper smiled at the headteacher and nodded. Ms Malignus turned to Mr Fields, who was sitting calmly in his chair.

"Rava." She motioned to him, "You too must feed, to ensure your duties are met." She walked over to where he was seated, the other teachers cowering as she passed. She handed him the bottle. "Only you and Helena may feed tonight." She walked away from him, to the staffroom door. "Now see this done," she growled, before stepping through and closing the door behind her, sneering as she heard the howls of anguish coming from the staffroom.

29.

It was growing dark by the time nine o'clock arrived. The evening was cool and pleasant. Sophie and Lucy walked up to the closed iron gates at the front of the school. There was a slight breeze, which made the branches of the old oak trees creak and groan gently.

Sophie pressed her face up against the railings and looked down the long drive towards the school. "It looks different in the dark, doesn't it?"

"It looks scary," Lucy replied. "Do you still think this is the right thing to do?"

Sophie turned and looked at her friend. "Yeah, I do," she answered immediately, "you saw them down in that cellar. We need to do this, Lucy."

"Ok," Lucy nodded, shivering slightly. They quietly waited, both lost in their thoughts, until they saw Jack approaching. He carried a black rucksack on his shoulders.

"What have you got in there?" Sophie asked him.

"Supplies," he answered with a shrug, feeling slightly embarrassed. "Torches and stuff, are you two ready?"

"Yeah," Sophie answered, "but how are we going to get in?"

"I've sorted that. I've left the window in the boys' toilet unlocked. We can push it open and get in that way," he grinned, "come on." He started to walk away from the gates, following the path that ran alongside the red brick wall and leaving the two girls where they stood.

"Where are you going, Jack?" Lucy asked.

He stopped and turned to answer her. "We can't get over the wall here, it's too open and anyone could see us. We'll be best going round to the fields at the back of the school and getting over there. No one will see us that way. Come on."

He turned around and carried on walking, the girls following. As they headed towards the fields, they tried to come up with some sort of plan for what they were about to do.

"We just get in and get out as fast as we can," Jack said. "Head straight to Malignus's office and straight down that tunnel, to the others."

"I've still got the key." Lucy said, patting her pocket. "But do you think we can get them out?"

Jack looked at her, confused. "What do you mean?"

"Well, you know," she began hesitantly. "What if they're…" She didn't finish the sentence.

"Dead?"

"They're not," Sophie interrupted quickly.

"How do you know?" Lucy asked.

"I just do. I can feel it," she answered. "They'll wake when we free them. They'll come out, don't worry." Lucy didn't respond.

"Look," Jack said as they walked along, "we don't know what will happen when we get down there but we've still got to try."

"Oy!" A shout came from behind them. All three stopped in their tracks and turned to see a figure running through the dark towards them. A sudden fear that they had been overheard and someone was running to stop them flushed through Jack.

"Ben!" Lucy exclaimed, breathing a sigh of relief as he got near. "I was worried who you might have been."

He looked at her as if she had said something strange. "Who did you think I was?" He laughed, out of breath from running. "I thought it was you three, I was worried I'd missed you. I've come to help," he said, smiling at them. "I'm sorry about what I said earlier and I don't know if what you say is true or not but that definitely wasn't Boz in class today. Can I help you?"

Lucy threw her arms around him. "Thank you. We need all the help we can get."

"Thanks," he chuckled.

Jack nodded and smiled at him. "Good to see you, mate," he said, relieved that it was Ben and not someone or something more sinister, "but we can't stay here all night. We've got to get a move on before it gets too late."

The daylight was quickly fading away as they walked and talked, filling Ben in on their plans and on what he'd find when they entered Malignus's office.

"Unbelievable," he said, shaking his head.

"Here we are," Jack said suddenly, as they reached the point he had been leading them to. They were in a farmer's field at the back of the school, near the red brick wall. On the other side of the wall was the small wood the school was named after. "No one will see us if we go over here. Everyone ok?" They all nodded. "Good, we jump over the wall and head straight to the Den. Then it's straight through to the boys' toilets and into the school." He took a deep breath. "If anyone wants to back out, then do it now." He paused for a moment as they stood in the darkness. No one moved or spoke. "Right, come on then." He walked over to the wall and leaned his back against it, making a cradle with his hands, to give somebody a leg up. "Ladies first?" he asked with a grin.

30.

One by one, they climbed over the wall and into the wood. The sunlight had completely gone and they huddled together in the oppressive darkness under the trees. The woods were quiet, save for the sound of the branches creaking in the breeze and the odd rustle of leaves as something scurried by in a hurry. "I've got two torches here," Jack whispered, rustling through his bag and pulling them out.

"What else have you got in there?" Ben asked, looking at the full rucksack.

"Just some stuff," Jack said, closing it quickly and handing a torch to Sophie. As carefully and as quietly as they could, they made their way through the bushes and trees and headed towards the school. As they reached the edge of the woods, Sophie suddenly stopped and turned her torch off.

"Quick Jack, turn it off," she said in a panic.

"What is it?" Lucy asked, suddenly filled with dread as Jack hurried to switch off the torch.

"Look," Sophie said, staring straight at the old building looming ahead of them, creepier than ever in the near-dark. "There are lights on in the school." At first no one spoke, they just stared. They could see that several of the windows were lit.

"Does anyone know if the place is empty?" Lucy asked. "Maybe they just left some of the lights on?"

"How could we know that?" Jack snapped. "I'd just assumed there'd be no one there."

"I think we should go back to the Den before we're seen," Ben suggested, "We'll sort out what we're going to do when we get back there." They all agreed and silently made their way back into the bush, Jack and Sophie turning their torches back on and shining them at the floor to light their way.

"Why would there be anyone in the school now?" Sophie whispered as they made their way back to the Den. "Don't the teachers have homes to go to?"

"I don't know," Lucy answered.

"It's not like they can have much work to do, is it?" Sophie continued grumbling as she walked, "all we ever do is copy out of books."

"Come to think of it, I don't think I've ever seen a teacher out of school," Ben said. "It's a bit weird, isn't it?"

"Never really thought about it before," Lucy mused. "They're always just there, aren't they? In fact, I don't think I've ever seen one turn up, or leave." They walked in single file, following the same path through the woods that they took every lunchtime.

A sense of dread started to creep over Sophie as she listened to what Lucy and Ben were saying. "Where's the car park?" she asked.

"What car park?"

"The teachers' one," she answered. "Surely there must be a car park for them."

Ben stopped walking, as if suddenly realising something. The others turned to look at him. "There isn't one," he answered.

"If there isn't a car park then where do they park when they get in? They won't all walk in, will they?" Sophie stated, not liking the implication they were slowly reaching.

"Shhh," Lucy suddenly hissed. "What was that noise?" All four of them stood and listened quietly.

"I can't hear anything," Jack whispered anxiously after a few moments. "It must be your imagination. You're making me…" But before he could finish his sentence, Lucy let out a terrible scream as a large shape came crashing through the bushes. It grabbed her roughly from behind, before she'd had chance to move, and began to drag her away from the group, back in the direction of the school. The woods were filled with the sounds of crashing branches as Lucy was violently dragged through the undergrowth, frightening the sleeping birds, whose squawks and calls mixed with the sounds of screaming as Lucy kicked and shouted out, trying to fight off whatever was holding her in this vice-like grip. She scratched and hit out at the arm that was holding onto her, doing everything she could to escape, and managed to squirm just enough to reach it with her mouth. She bit down upon it as hard as she could. It let out a horrific, animalistic shriek and dropped Lucy to the floor.

Lucy rolled away and looked up to see the muscular, bulking figure of Miss Betteridge, holding her arm and glaring, spittle hanging from her mouth and her face full of fury and vengeance.

Miss Betteridge slowly licked her arm where she had been bitten, her eyes never leaving Lucy's, and was about to rush towards her when she was hit by a cloud of white powder. She paused for a moment, as if registering what had happened, before grabbing her face and falling to her knees, muffled screams coming from behind her hands.

Lucy looked behind to see Jack standing over her, holding something. Betteridge was now lying on the floor, crumpled and shaking. Jack held out his hand to Lucy. He was breathing heavily and trembling as he helped her slowly to her feet. She hugged him hard.

"What did you do?" she asked as they looked down at the teacher writhing on the floor in pain, shaking with panic and fear. They watched as Betteridge's convulsions gradually began to slow.

"I… I… just threw it at her," Jack replied, his voice trembling. "I couldn't see you but could hear you and then all of a sudden you were there and I just grabbed it out of my bag and threw it at her."

"What did you throw?" Lucy asked, still shaking.

"This." He held out the object. It was an open box of table salt. "I just had it in my bag… it's from home. All this talk of Golems and the weird stuff we saw in that cellar, well it got me thinking… I saw this programme on the telly and they were using salt for protection against ghosts and things so I just brought it… you know. Just in case."

Just then, they heard a rustling coming from behind them. Jack spun around quickly, ready to hit whatever came out of the bushes.

"Whoa," Ben shouted as he and Sophie came crashing out of the undergrowth. "It's us." Sophie grabbed Lucy and hugged her.

"Lucy, what happened? I heard you scream and then you were gone. We couldn't find either of you."

"It was Betteridge. Look," Lucy pointed at the body, curled up and lying on the floor. It had stopped shaking and was now very still. "Jack saved me."

"She must have gotten lost or disorientated in the woods," Jack said quickly, "and ended up coming in a circle back to me."

Ben slowly walked over to the body and prodded it with his foot. It began to bubble.

"Is she dead?" Jack asked.

"Look," Ben replied. The body had started to melt away into piles of gloop.

"I'm going to be sick," Jack said, turning away.

Sophie walked over to look at the body. "What happened?" she asked, looking at the gloopy mess that was now forming on the ground.

"Jack threw salt at her," Lucy answered.

"Salt?" Ben asked, leaning in to get a better look at the melting figure. There was now more melted mess and gloop than actual body. The stench was horrendous and he pulled away, making a face. "Nice work, Jack. What made you use salt, though? It's like melting a slug." He moved away from the pool of bile.

"Just something I saw on telly," Jack answered, shrugging his shoulders and refusing to look at the rapidly melting Miss Betteridge.

Lucy picked up a small branch and approached what remained of the teacher, giving it a prod. "Don't know about a slug but whatever it is it's not human," she said, both surprised and scared by what she was looking at.

"So what is it?" Sophie asked.

"Some sort of monster," Jack said, looking at them solemnly, still holding the salt in his hand. They stood silently for a moment, looking at the pile of goo in front of them.

"We've got to go before something else arrives," Ben said eventually, turning away from the mess. They kept their torches off and began walking through the woods, back to the wall.

"How did you know?" Sophie asked Jack.

"Know what?" he answered, not looking at her but at the floor. Lucy and Ben were both silent.

"That they were monsters? I mean that Betteridge wasn't human," she stuttered.

"I didn't really," he muttered back to her. "I just kinda thought, what if...? You know, what if there's something else going on."

"What do you mean?" she asked, slightly confused.

"Well, it was when you said about those Golems. They're not supposed to be real, are they? Yet here we are looking at them in class and I thought what if other things were real... you know, like monsters?" He looked up at her and she smiled at him. "So I just put as many things as I could think of in my bag."

"Well, I'm glad you did," Lucy said, having listened to their conversation. "Thanks, Jack."

"Yes. Thank you, Jack," Sophie smiled. She couldn't see that he was blushing in the darkness.

They continued walking, Ben silently leading the group until they reached the wall. There, they stood in a circle, surrounded by nothing but darkness. Lucy flinched at every noise she heard coming from the woods, half expecting another figure to come crashing out at them. She linked Jack's arm with hers and gently squeezed it.

"This is wrong," Sophie whispered, looking at the group. "We can't just give up."

"Sophie, I've just melted a teacher," Jack said, staring back at her. "Whatever else she was, she was still a teacher. We can't just hang around here."

"No, Jack. Sophie's right," Lucy said, looking at him, trembling slightly, "we can't just give up and whatever that was, it wasn't a human."

"They're right, Jack," Ben said thoughtfully. "That thing wasn't human. But it was definitely Betteridge and if she

… it … whatever we call it, was there then we can guess the other teachers will be there, too. Whatever they are." There was a silence. "What do you think will happen when they find she's missing and see that mess?"

An unspoken answer hung between all of them. Sophie shivered in the dark. "That wasn't a human, it was a monster," she said forcefully. "And we can't leave Tom, Boz or any of the others to these monsters."

"We have to go back and stop this," Lucy said quietly.

Jack was still holding his packet of salt and felt his grip tighten. He was glad he had watched all of those scary films and he was glad he'd packed his bag… just in case!

31.

They huddled together in the dark, under the trees. Lucy and Sophie comforted each other while Jack leaned against the red brick wall, happy for the break.

Ben looked at him. "Right, Jack," he said, trying not to sound as frightened as he actually felt. "Before we go any further, we need to know what else you've got in your bag." Jack nodded his head and they all gathered around him whilst he took his bag from his shoulders. He crouched down and opened it up.

"Well, obviously there's the torches," he began, pleased with himself for having brought his bag of stuff with him. "And the salt," he continued, "that was for the ghosts."

"Ghosts?" Ben interrupted. "You thought we might have seen ghosts?" Lucy hit him in the arm.

"Well, yeah," Jack answered, blushing slightly, glad that he couldn't be seen in the dark, "I didn't know what we'd see, did I? So I just packed it," he answered slightly defensively, "and it's a good job I did as we now know it works on the teachers, don't we?"

"Teacher," Sophie corrected him.

"What do you mean, Soph?" Lucy asked.

"It worked on Betteridge. But that doesn't mean it'll work on any of the others, does it?" She looked at Jack, feeling slightly awkward. "I'm sorry, Jack, but we don't even know what these things are, do we?"

"That's ok, Sophie," he replied. "And you're right, we've got no idea what they are, or what will work. I got lucky with Betteridge and the salt but we might not be so lucky next time, with any of the others." He returned to pulling items out of his bag. "Garlic," he said, holding up a string of garlic bulbs, "for vampires." He took out two cricket stumps, which were flat at one end but sharply pointed at the other. "Stakes of wood," he said, "I've sharpened the ends for driving through the heart." He put them on the floor and took out a bottle of clear water.

"Water?" Ben asked.

"Holy water," Jack replied, looking up at him. "It's from my grandad's, he's always going to Mass and is really religious. I didn't think it would hurt bringing it. Oh, and this." He took out a silver crucifix, which hung from a silver chain. He put both items on the floor, next to the cricket stumps and garlic chain.

"Deodorant?" Lucy asked, looking over his shoulder into the bag.

"No, it's a homemade flame-thrower," he replied. He took the deodorant and a long, thin lighter out of his bag. "Watch this," he grinned as he lit the lighter and sprayed the deodorant over the flame, creating a huge plume of fire that lit up the darkness around them. He quickly stopped spraying when he saw their confused faces. "Fire?" he mumbled, ignoring their bewildered expressions, "well, it worked on Frankenstein." He grinned, adding the items to the growing pile on the floor.

"Anything else in there?" Lucy asked, simultaneously impressed at his preparedness and slightly scared.

"Yeah," Jack answered, pulling a large iron spanner from the bag. "There's this." He held it out in front of his face.

Ben took it from him and smacked it down into the palm of his own hand. "Nice," he said, "what's this for?"

"Hitting things with." Jack answered, grinning at him. He smiled at them all and looked proudly at his stuff. "That's the lot; your very own monster survival kit, right there. Most definitely not to be used on real people or teachers, only on monsters!"

"Well done, mate," Ben said, nodding his head, impressed with Jack's foresight. "Do you mind if I keep hold of this?" he asked, swinging the spanner around.

"No, mate," Jack answered with a smile, feeling pleased with himself. "Do you guys want to take something?" he asked the girls.

"Can I have the salt?" Lucy asked, thinking about her previous encounter with Miss Betteridge, "and one of those cricket stumps?" Jack handed them over. "Do you want the other one, Sophie?" he asked.

"Yes, please," she answered. "Can I have the holy water, too?"

"Sure," he replied. He put the torches, garlic and crucifix back in his bag but held on to his home-made flame-thrower. "No torches?" he asked, looking for approval, "they might show us up if anyone looks through a window." The others agreed with him. "Are we ready then?"

Sophie took a deep breath. "Yeah."

"Me too," said Ben. "Lucy, are you ok?"

"Yeah," she answered putting her hand in her pocket and taking out the key. They all looked at it, knowing where it had come from and the secrets it protected. "Jack, take this," she said, trying to hand it to him.

"No, Lucy," he protested. "You keep hold of that."

"I don't want it," she insisted, pushing it into his hands. "I hate having it." He looked at her thoughtfully. "Anyway, you're the one who came prepared. You're the one with the stuff, so you're the one who should have the key."

"Ok," he answered after a moment's thought. He took the key from her and put it in his pocket. He smiled, trying to show that he felt confident and brave, but deep inside he was terrified at the thought of going into the school. A hush fell over the group. The evening breeze, which had been so pleasant earlier, seemed to have grown stronger and colder. It bit into them as they stood in the woods. They looked at each other, their nerves starting to eat away at them now they knew there could be monsters to fight. They needed to focus on their task again before anybody changed their mind. "The window to the boys' toilet is open," Jack said, focusing them all on a practical subject, "we head for there. Once we're in, we head straight for Malignus's office. Stay together, though; we don't know if there'll be anyone looking out but we have to assume that there will be and that Betteridge wasn't alone." The others nodded in agreement. "We keep the noise down and keep as close as we can."

They set off, creeping through the dark woods as silently as they could, across the fields and up to the school.

32.

The window to the boys' toilet squeaked loudly as Jack lowered it shut. The sound echoed off the tiled walls, making them wince. They had made their way across the fields and into the school without any further incident, and without seeing any other teachers. They waited several minutes, listening for sounds of approaching teachers who may have been alerted by the squealing window. The tension was unbearable.

"Do boys' toilets always smell this bad?" Lucy whispered, holding her nose theatrically, trying to lighten the mood.

Jack stifled a laugh. "Very funny," he whispered, "I bet you the girls' loos smell like roses, don't they?"

Lucy smiled at him. "You know, this would be quite exciting if it wasn't so scary," she whispered. He grinned back.

"You two, stop messing around and concentrate," Ben hissed. He and Sophie were by the door. Sophie had her hand on the door knob and was about to open it. Jack and Lucy crept across to join them.

Sophie opened the door slightly and peered out, to make sure no one was on the other side. When she was confident they were safe, she waved them through. "Keep your eyes open for anything," she whispered as they slipped past her, through the door.

The corridor was pitch-black. Ben led the way, Sophie tucked in close behind him, followed by Jack, with Lucy bringing up the rear. The school could be a foreboding and scary place during the day but at night it became even more so. Every shadow seemed to be filled with lingering danger and every noise seemed magnified, bouncing off the walls. They made their way as stealthily as they could. Ben could barely see in front of his face and felt as though he were stumbling blindly through the darkness. Occasionally, they passed a room which had its lights on but generally the corridors were deserted and dark. They crouched low as they made their way through the school, trying to remain as hidden as possible from any eyes that might see them. Each time they reached an open door or a corner, Ben would stop and listen for any indication of a teacher in their path.

Lucy winced at every sound she could hear and wondered if the others were doing the same. As they progressed through the school she kept glancing behind her to make sure they weren't being followed. Suddenly, she froze. She was sure she had just seen something move at the far end of the corridor they had just come through. She crouched low, staying as still as she could, and peered into the darkness, unsure of what she had seen. It happened again. A shape had definitely moved. She reached out, trying to alert Jack, but there was no one there. She quickly spun round to grab him, taking her eyes from the moving shape behind them, but he had gone. He, Sophie and Ben hadn't noticed when she had stopped and had carried on moving forward, creeping through the school towards Malignus's office. Lucy froze, not knowing what to do. Her heart and mind were racing but her body remained firmly rooted to the spot.

Slowly, the shape began to move closer; began to form an outline. It was a person. A person was heading towards her. A million questions swam through Lucy's mind. Who was it? Did it know they were there? Had it been following them? Could she escape without being seen? She tried to move, to get away, but her legs wouldn't budge as the fear had crept into them. All she could do was make herself as small and as quiet as she possibly could. She quickly looked for somewhere to hide and spotted a small bookcase further up the corridor. If she could make it there she might be able to hide behind it. It took all of her effort to move herself to it but she got there. She pushed herself into the corner, between the bookcase and the wall, and closed her eyes. She slowed her breathing and waited.

At first, there was only silence, aside from the sound of her own heart beating wildly in her chest. Soon, though, she began to hear something else. The soft sound of someone shuffling their feet coming towards her along the corridor. It was imperceptible at first but gradually began to grow louder, until it felt as though it were right on top of her. Then she heard the wheezing and grunting of whoever it was. Lucy felt completely alone and vulnerable, and wanted to run, to cry out and escape from her hiding place, but she couldn't. All she could do was sit still and remain as hidden from view as she could.

The grunting and shuffling feet abruptly stopped. Lucy held her breath and slowly opened one eye to see Mr Parkes standing directly opposite where she was hiding. He seemed to be different, though. He was wheezing and grunting loudly and seemed to be sleepy and not quite alert, as he swayed wearily on the spot before her. He reminded her of how the Watchouts were on the yard at lunchtime. His arms hung limp by his side and his head lolled backwards and forwards, as though he were fighting off sleep. Lucy held the cricket stump Jack had given her in one hand and the salt in the other. She could feel her grip on the stump tighten as she watched the teacher, who was absently staring ahead, into some unseen distance before him. *Move on, move on*, she silently urged as she could feel her breath beginning to run out. Just as she thought she couldn't hold it any longer, he began to shuffle forwards again. It was as though it was taking all of his effort to simply move. Lucy could feel her lungs bursting. She couldn't hold her breath any longer. As quietly as she could, she took a breath, constantly watching the teacher, who was shuffling away from her, for any reaction. She was just beginning to relax a little when she saw him stop. She instantly tensed up and held her breath again. He shook his head and sniffed the air. He sniffed it again and again, as though he were an animal who had found a scent but couldn't pinpoint it, becoming more and more agitated when he suddenly stopped, his nose pointed up high in the air. He took one last, long sniff and slowly turned around. Lucy closed her eyes and tried to push herself further into the darkness. All was silent, she could no longer hear Mr Parkes moving or breathing. *Don't look, don't look*, she thought, petrified.

Suddenly, she felt a hand grab her by the hair and lift her off her feet. A second hand quickly clapped itself over her face, covering her nose and mouth. She was hoisted up into the air and pinned against the wall, dropping the wooden cricket stump and salt in surprise as she was lifted up. She kicked out and hit him as hard as she could, grabbing at Mr Parkes and scratching his face. He let go of her, trying to protect himself from her desperate clawing and she dropped to the floor, her hand landing on the packet of salt, which she grabbed and instinctively threw at him as hard as she could. The salt exploded in his face and he roared in anger and pain, trying to brush it out of his beard and hair. The more he brushed and pulled at it, though, the deeper it fell in, scorching him wherever it touched his skin. He grunted and whined as the salt burned, momentarily forgetting about Lucy.

She scrambled across to where the cricket stump had rolled and made a grab for it. She could hear Mr Parkes stumbling towards her, howling with rage, and rolled onto her back, holding the stump out in front just as he threw himself upon her, the sharp end crashing through his chest and impaling him as he landed heavily on it. He let out a high-pitched scream and instantly exploded like a pricked balloon. Ooze, gunk and plasma flew in every direction, covering the floor and the walls, and Lucy, who lay coughing and spluttering, still holding the wooden stake out in front of her.

Her ears were ringing from the explosion and she lay still on the floor for a moment, trying to figure out what had just happened, before slowly sitting up. Ooze and slime covered her from head to foot. She wiped her eyes and shook her head, and was putting her fingers in her ears, trying to clear them, when she heard a noise. Footsteps. Running towards her, getting faster and louder the closer they came. She tried to push herself to her feet but couldn't. All her energy and resolve had vanished. She tensed and sat there in the dark, in the slime and ooze, waiting for whatever was making the noise to arrive.

33.

$\mathcal{B}$en, Jack and Sophie appeared in front of her. Lucy breathed a sigh of relief. She was still dazed and covered in all of the mess that had once been Mr Parkes, but she smiled and relaxed slightly when she saw her friends.

"Lucy, what the…?" Sophie stuttered, kneeling on the floor next to her friend and hugging her, ignoring the gunk she was covered in.

"You weren't there!" Jack spluttered quickly, his face white with panic and filled with fear. "You weren't there! I looked back and you weren't there!" He grabbed Lucy's hand and pulled her to her feet. Sophie put her hand on her back, as though to keep her upright. "Where did you go?" Jack stammered, hugging Lucy tightly.

"Lucy, what's all this?" Sophie asked, feeling the ooze that was now spread all over her clothes.

"It's everywhere," Jack said, realising that he was standing in it and now, thanks to his hug, it was stuck to him as well.

"Mr Parkes," Lucy whispered.

"What?" Sophie asked, wiping at herself.

"It's Mr Parkes, all of it," Lucy answered nervously, gunk dripping from her hair. Jack stepped away from the ooze he had been standing in and began urgently wiping it off him.

"We've got to go," whispered Ben, who had been keeping a look-out down the corridors. "If we heard that scream, you can guarantee someone else would have heard it as well. We've got to move."

The others stared at him. An eerie silence seemed to grow in the corridor as they listened out for any sign of approaching danger.

"Back to the woods," Ben said as quietly as he could. "We can sort out what happened when we're safe."

The others followed Ben as he led the way back down the corridor towards the boys' toilets. This time, Jack followed Sophie and Lucy, making sure he was at the rear and nobody went missing. At every corner and doorway they checked to make sure they were all together, and quickly reached the toilets without any further incident. They entered the room, ready to climb back through the window and to the relative safety of the woods, when they heard it. As Jack closed the door, a hideous howl filled the corridors. It seemed to bounce off each wall, cutting the children deep to their bones. They froze, almost hypnotised by the raw, guttural cry.

"What was that?" Lucy whispered, still full of fear.

"It's one of them," Sophie whispered back, her voice trembling. "They must've found Parkes."

Ben headed to the window and opened it. The squeak sounded as loud to them as the howl had.

"Quickly, before we're found," he growled, climbing through into the dark of the night. Jack helped the girls before climbing through last, closing the window behind him as quietly as he could. He looked at Lucy, who was waiting next to him, covered in ooze and mess and shaking with fear. He was shivering and tried to steady himself.

"Come on," Ben whispered, leading the way across the field back to the wood. They were running as quickly as they could, eager to get away, when they heard the howl again. This time, it was louder. It was as if whatever was making it was following them. They clambered into the bushes on the edge of the wood but Jack suddenly skidded to a stop. He could hear a noise; a grunting, snuffling sort of noise, a bit like heavy breathing. He listened with all of his concentration, trying to locate the source of the horrible sound, before turning to see a large figure running towards them. It was breathing heavily and struggling to keep up with them. He stopped and crouched down, watching the figure get closer, hoping he hadn't been seen. The other three hadn't noticed him stop and he didn't dare call them. He watched as they disappeared through the undergrowth and steadied his breathing. He shook the can of deodorant he had brought and held the lighter out in readiness, his finger hovering over the trigger, ready to spark a flame if he had to.

The figure grew nearer and nearer and then stopped. Jack watched unseen as the fat frame of Mrs Thomass waited just in front of him. He didn't move as he watched her trying to see through the growth into the trees. She was breathing very heavily and seemed to be struggling to catch her breath. *Come on*, he thought to himself, crouching on his knees as still as he could, *just a bit closer*. She didn't move and just stood there, searching for them and peering into the darkness of the woods. After a few minutes, she gave up, turned around, and waddled slowly away. Jack waited until he couldn't see her anymore, before quietly standing up and making his way back to the wall, where he knew his friends would be waiting.

He could see Sophie and Lucy looking out anxiously for him. They seemed relieved when he reached them.

"Jack, where have you…?" Lucy began but Jack quickly stopped her.

"Shh," he hissed, putting his fingers to his lips. "They're in the woods. We've got to go now."

One by one, they quietly climbed over the wall and into the field behind. "We are never doing that again," Lucy said finally, hugging Jack as he jumped down from the wall. He returned her hug.

"We can't talk here," he said, holding on to her. "My mom's still at work. Get back to mine and we can talk there." He looked at the ooze that was covering her and was now on him again, "Lucy, you can have a shower, too." He wiped his top down. She smiled at him and took his hand, holding it tightly as they walked along the perimeter of the wall. They remained silent, listening out for any sound that might hint that they were being pursued, levels of tension and anxiety slowly falling as they eventually left the field.

"Thank you," Lucy said quietly, smiling at Jack.

"What for?"

"You saved me from them," she answered, looking at him softly. He shrugged his shoulders. Sophie and Ben walked behind them.

"I think she likes him," Ben whispered to Sophie, nodding at Lucy and Ben.

Sophie smiled and nodded in agreement. "Probably. Him saving her life might just do that." She grinned.

There was a chill in the air as they walked in silence, each lost in thoughts of what had happened and subconsciously letting their feet lead their way. They only stopped when they had reached the front of the school and the large iron gates.

Jack looked at the old building, the trees along the driveway swaying in the breeze and the dark silhouettes of the gargoyles across the roof seeming to be staring at them. "Funny," he laughed quietly to Lucy. "It looks so dark and quiet from here. You'd never know."

She squeezed his arm. "But we do know," she whispered, pulling him away.

34.

Malignus was furious. She grabbed one of her teachers by his hair and threw him across the staffroom. She grabbed another and pushed him through a cupboard door, the contents falling all over him as he slumped to the ground. "How could you?" she screamed at all of them. "They are just small, weak little children and they somehow manage to evade you all?" She raged at them and stepped imperiously across the staffroom, in her fury punishing all; kicking those who were lying prone on the floor and standing on others as she passed them. They all tried to hide from her, to escape her wrath, cowering under tables and hiding behind anything they could find as she took her anger out on anyone who crossed her path. "You fools!" she screamed. "You useless imbeciles!" She stopped only when she heard the staffroom door open, spinning suddenly around on her heels, ready to grab and punish whoever came through it. She stopped instantly and froze when she saw who it was.

"Veronica," smiled Mrs Harper, glaring at her sharply over the rim of her small, round glasses. She glanced around the room, surveying the mess and carnage surrounding the headteacher. "Rava and I would like a word. In your office." She smiled again, a cold certainty flickering in her smile, and without waiting for a response turned around and walked back through the door, leaving it open for the headteacher to follow.

Malignus's eyes widened and her nostrils flared with anger. "How dare they…!" she fumed. "How dare they presume to command me…!" She pressed the heel of her boot into the stomach of one of the teachers at her feet, before storming out of the staffroom and following Mrs Harper.

By the time she reached her office, Ms Malignus had managed to compose herself. Mrs Harper and Mr Fields were of a different caste to the others and Ms Malignus knew their value to the Academy, even if Fields was a male. It wouldn't be wise or prudent to needlessly anger or upset them. She walked through her door to find that they had both already seated themselves in front of her desk.

"Please sit down," Mrs Harper instructed with a smile, indicating the large headteacher's chair, which Ms Malignus usually sat in. Malignus bit her tongue. She didn't like being invited to sit in her own chair, in her own office.

Mrs Harper smiled at her whilst Mr Fields appeared to be dozing. "As you may be aware," Mrs Harper began, "there has been an intrusion tonight." She stared at Ms Malignus, still smiling but with a steely seriousness in her eyes. "We still have staff searching the school and the grounds but we know that there has been at least one fatality." Ms Malignus bristled in her seat while Mrs Harper carried on talking. "It is safe to make the assumption that tonight's intrusion has been made by the same children whom you believe have been… ah, what was it now?" She opened a small notebook that she had been holding and flicked through its pages, stopping at the appropriate place. "Ah yes, here we are," she continued, smiling broadly and reading from the book, "by the children who have 'roamed unobserved' and have been 'caught out of lessons'." She closed the book and watched the headteacher, looking for any reaction. "Veronica, I'm sure I don't need to say this but you do realise the importance of, and need for, secrecy?" Ms Malignus curtly nodded her head, her blood and anger beginning to rise again. "It is my sacred duty as a trusted keeper of records to remind you that should these children, or anyone else, find out about our operation, the consequences will be most serious." Mrs Harper held Ms Malignus's stare. She could see the fury that was brewing inside the headteacher and was enjoying the authority that her caste had given her. She knew that in this situation she was untouchable and could provoke and goad Ms Malignus as much as she wanted. It was her role to observe and record; Malignus would be the one who would be held solely accountable. There was a knock at the door. "Come," Mrs Harper called, still smiling at Ms Malignus. Miss Thomass waddled into the room and looked at the figures sitting around the table. She didn't know who to address; Mrs Harper, who had called her into the room, or her headteacher. She decided to look at neither and instead looked at the floor. "Please forgive my intrusssion," she whispered, "we have found the remainss of another in the school groundsss."

The tension in Ms Malignus was palpable. "Who?" she growled through gritted teeth.

"We believe it to be Misss Betteridge, Headmissstresss," mumbled Miss Thomass to the floor. An uncomfortable silence filled the room.

"You may go," Mrs Harper said briskly, to Miss Thomass. Without saying another word, she opened her notebook and made a note in its pages. She looked up at the headteacher. "That now makes two," she said with a menace in her voice, her smile momentarily missing.

"Combine this with the wandering children and it does not make for pleasant reading." She closed her book and stood up. Mr Fields suddenly seemed to wake up and stood next to her. They walked over to the door. "Ensure that this is addressed, Veronica," Mrs Harper said, staring at the Head with a finality in her voice before she politely nodded and walked out of the room, followed by Mr Fields.

Ms Malignus stood behind her desk, staring at the door, not speaking. Her rage continued to build. *How dare they presume?* she thought, angrily. *How dare they order me?* She screamed and in one massive explosion of rage and temper she flipped the large oak table onto its side.

"How dare they!" she yelled into the empty room.

35.

Lucy smiled as the warm water flowed over her. She ran the shampoo through her hair, washing away the last remnants of Mr Parkes, and watched as the ooze and muck flowed away down the drain. She couldn't believe the night they'd had, and shuddered when she thought of what might have happened. She'd had two fearsome encounters with both Parkes and Betteridge. Who knew what might have happened to her, had they managed to catch her? Only they hadn't, and she had Jack to thank for that. She smiled when she thought of him and clung on to that thought, letting the water wash away the horrible feelings of the night.

The others were all waiting for her in Jack's bedroom. Ben was sitting on the floor, leaning against the edge of Jack's bed, which Sophie was sitting cross-legged upon. Jack was on the chair next to the small desk in the corner of the room. He and Sophie had both got changed and she was now wearing one of his jumpers. As Lucy's clothes had been covered in the grime from Mr Parkes, Jack had offered to clean them in his washing machine, along with his and Sophie's dirty tops. He had lent Lucy a pair of tracksuit bottoms and a sweater. They didn't quite fit her and she felt odd wearing them but strangely comfortable at the same time. He smiled at her as she sat on the bed next to Sophie. "We were just talking about what

163

happened," he said. "You did well getting away from Parkes."

She shook her head at him; she didn't want to be reminded of what had happened. "I didn't do well," she said, feeling upset, "I killed a teacher!"

"No, you didn't," Sophie interrupted, "and we've got to stop thinking of them... those things... as teachers; as people, even, because they're not. They're monsters, all of them."

"I know that," Lucy argued, "but still, it's not nice, is it, and it's definitely not a good thing."

"Nobody's saying it is, Lucy," Ben interrupted, "but if you didn't stop him, God knows what he would've done to you."

"You'd have ended up down in that horrible cellar," Sophie said, desperately trying to get through to her friend. "You did the only thing you could have done."

Lucy pulled her legs up to her chin. "I still killed him," she protested, "you don't know what that's like."

Sophie looked at Ben for support but he sat quietly.

"No, they don't, but I do," Jack said, his tone dark and grim, staring at Lucy, who had hidden her face behind her knees. "I know how you're feeling, Luce, believe me I do. But you know they're right. We can't think of them as humans because they're not. They're monsters. That's what they are, monsters." They all sat silently, each lost in their own thoughts about the monsters in the school and what had happened or what could have happened to them that evening.

After a while, Ben asked the question they had all been thinking. "What happens now?"

"They'll know what we've done, won't they?" Sophie asked, looking at her feet. "They'll come for us."

"No, they won't," Jack interrupted. Sophie and Ben look at him curiously.

"What do you mean?" Sophie asked him.

"Well, how will they know it was us?" he replied. The others all looked at him, silently waiting for him to expand upon what he was suggesting. "I mean, who exactly saw us?"

"No one," Ben answered. "At least, no one that we know of."

"Betteridge and Parkes did," Lucy muttered quietly under her breath.

Jack laughed out loud. "Exactly." He chuckled, "And I don't think either of those two will say anything, do you?" He winked at Lucy and gave her a smile. She smiled back at him, her mood lifting slightly.

"What about Thomass?" Ben asked. "You said she had followed us into the wood. Could she have seen who we were?"

"No, I seriously doubt it," Jack answered. "She was struggling to keep up with us. She could barely breathe, by the sounds of her, and could never have seen anything which would have given us away in the dark, and from that distance." He looked at the others confidently. "She gave up looking because she had no idea what or who she was looking for. I wouldn't worry about her giving any descriptions, or anything like that."

"Ok then, we don't have any concerns about that. But I'll say it again: what happens now?" Ben asked.

"I can't go back there," Lucy said quickly. "Not after tonight."

"We have to, Lucy," Sophie said softly, leaning towards her friend and putting her arms around her. She pulled her close and Lucy rested her head into her, feeling comforted slightly. "If we don't go back in, they'll definitely suspect us. We've got to remember, they will still be looking for whoever it was."

"We have to act as normally as we can," Jack said.

"But we can't just leave Tom and the others," Sophie said suddenly, jumping at Jack's comment. "We can't just pretend that nothing is happening."

"I didn't mean that, Sophie," he replied earnestly. "I just meant we go in to school as normal."

Lucy suddenly sat up and looked at Sophie as though she had just realised something. "You're right. Normal," she said, grinning excitedly as an idea was starting to form.

Sophie looked at her, confused. "Yeah...?" she said, surprised at the sudden upbeat turn and excited look that Lucy was now giving her.

"Normal. That's it," Lucy repeated, smiling at her friend.

"What are you two going on about?" Ben asked. Sophie shrugged her shoulders.

"Think about it." Lucy replied. "When is the only time we ever know where all the staff are, even Malignus?"

"Lunch," Jack answered.

"She'll never leave her office empty now though, will she?" Ben interrupted. "Even at lunch."

"Especially when she knows someone's been in there," Jack agreed, shaking his head.

"But it's not though, is it?" Lucy insisted, smiling at them all. "Lunch isn't the only time, is it? Come on, think 'normal'." She looked at them excitedly.

The boys looked confused but Sophie's eyes began to widen and she began to grow as excited as Lucy. "The only other time I've ever seen them all together is..." she began.

"Exactly." Lucy interrupted. grinning at her. "Normal."

"Exactly what?" Ben said, beginning to grow frustrated. "Can one of you two please fill me in here?"

"What does Malignus 'normally' do when she's caught a kid?" Lucy began.

"Or when she's wanted to catch someone and is looking for them?" Sophie interrupted, smiling at Lucy.

"Come on, think will you," Lucy shouted at the boys. She threw a pillow at Jack, hitting him in the head. Both of the girls were now sitting bolt upright on the edge of the bed. "When she caught James and Ben. When she was looking for Tom. Even when she just wants to shout at a kid, any kid."

"Like a kid in red shoes," Sophie prompted.

Jack slowly started to realise what they were referring to. "Assembly," he whispered. Lucy beamed at him.

"Assembly?" Ben asked, still confused.

"Yeah," Lucy said, grinning. "She 'normally' has an assembly whenever she's looking for someone, or has something to say, doesn't she? And we know she'll be looking for someone now."

"And you can bet she'll have something to say tomorrow," Sophie chimed in excitedly.

"She'll call an assembly, first thing tomorrow morning," Lucy looked around at the group. "Every teacher and every pupil will be in the hall."

"Thomass won't," Jack interrupted.

"She never leaves that office," Ben said, agreeing with him.

"And what if there's someone else who isn't in there?" Jack continued, beginning to see where Lucy was taking this. "If you're suggesting what I think you're suggesting, what if we're wrong? What if she's more cautious tomorrow, after everything that's happened tonight, and keeps staff out of the hall?"

"It won't matter," Sophie said, grinning. "We'll be ok."

"How will we be ok?" Ben spluttered, finally catching up with the girls' plan. "Anyone not in the assembly will be done for."

"Not everyone." Sophie grinned at Lucy, who was grinning back at her.

Ben looked at Jack. "Do you know what they're going on about?" he asked.

Jack shrugged his shoulders. "Not got a clue, mate."

Both of the boys looked at the girls, who were clearly enjoying teasing them.

Lucy laughed, "Prefects won't get in trouble, will they?"

"Prefects? Of course!" Jack joined in, suddenly becoming as excited as the girls. "You two are brilliant."

Ben still looked confused.

"We're all prefects, aren't we?" Sophie laughed. "We have got the badges after all."

"We pinched some prefect badges from Harper," Lucy said, turning to Ben. "Don't you see? Tomorrow we put the badges on, then during assembly when Malignus has called everybody into the hall, we, as prefects, will be able to walk straight into her office and free all the kids in the cellar. No one will stop us because they'll think we're prefects sent to patrol the school." She smiled at him, then turned to face Jack. For the first time, she thought they might actually be able to succeed.

36.

The next morning, the spring sun was shining and there wasn't a cloud in the sky. It was set to be a beautiful day, almost as if summer had arrived prematurely. They met early outside the school gates, as they had agreed the night before; anxious but excited about what was to come.

"Is everyone clear with the plan?" Sophie asked, nervously talking at a million miles an hour as she handed the small orange prefect badges out. They each nodded, taking their badges. "Remember, don't put them on until the assembly. It's too risky, wearing them now. And act like the prefects do. You know, like all zombie and weird. Who has the key?" she said quickly, suddenly panicking and looking at Lucy.

"I haven't got it," Lucy said sharply.

"I've got it," Jack answered, taking it out of his pocket and showing it to them. "We're not going to need it, though," he said, putting it back in his pocket. "Remember, the cupboard door isn't locked," he said, looking at Lucy. He smiled and winked at her. "When we went in there it was already open and if you think about it, Malignus won't have been able to lock it because we've had the key." He grinned at them. "That cupboard will have been unlocked this whole time. Which I reckon will have driven her mental." He laughed, "Anyone at any time could have opened the cupboard and found out her little secret."

"Well, I'll try not to feel too sorry for her," Sophie said sharply.

Lucy punched Jack in the arm, smiling at him. "Just make sure you bring it, just in case." She laughed.

The four of them stood for a moment and looked at each other. The laughs and smiles faded away as the seriousness of the situation crept up on them. "If we're all clear on what to do, we'd best get on with it," Sophie said eventually, her smile now replaced with a resolute determination. "Good luck," she said, picking up her school bag and turning to walk away.

"Oh wait," Jack said suddenly, "I nearly forgot." He picked up his backpack and opened it. "They worked last night so I thought why not bring them today; you never know, do you?" He began to hand out packets of salt. "Like my old grandad used to say, 'You're better off having it but not needing it, than needing it but not having it.'" He grinned.

"No thanks, mate, I've brought my own," Ben said, smirking and opening his bag, showing them the contents. "Salt, that spanner you gave me last night, and my mom's crucifix. Proper monster-killing equipment." He laughed. Jack grinned back at him and handed the salt packets to the girls. He then reached into his bag. It still contained the deodorant can flame-thrower and silver crucifix and chain. He had also packed other items and pulled two water pistols out, which he gave to the girls.

"Holy water," he said, "I've weaponised it." They laughed and Lucy gave him a hug.

"Thanks, Jack," she kissed him lightly on the cheek. He blushed and looked away from them.

Sophie smiled at Lucy. "I'll see you all in the corridor," she said, putting Jack's gifts in her bag. "Good luck, everyone." She turned away and walked through the school gates onto the long drive. As she walked she looked at the imposing school in front of her and shivered.

As usual, Mrs French was waiting when they arrived in class. Sophie couldn't believe how bad she looked. The stale, musty smell which usually filled the room was worse than it had ever been and Mrs French looked as though she had been up all night and hadn't had a minute's sleep. She sat on her chair behind her desk, shoulders hunched forward and head resting on her large double chin, staring into the space ahead. She seemed dazed and confused and didn't seem to notice the class entering the room. *Good*, Sophie thought as she looked at her, *I hope you've been up all night looking for us.* She smiled ever so slightly as she looked at the toad-like teacher, but not enough for anyone else to notice.

The children stood patiently behind their chairs waiting for Mrs French to tell them to be seated but she just sat there, blankly staring into the middle distance. No one dared sit down until they had been told to and some of them started to fidget, unsure what to do. Eventually, one of the boys cleared his throat in an exaggerated manner, attempting to draw her attention to them. It worked. Mrs French seemed to snap to, as if suddenly realising they were there. "Sit," she croaked at them. Her voice sounded sore and dry, as if it were hurting her to speak. She looked at the class angrily. Sophie couldn't help but notice the hate and greed on her face. Mrs French licked her lips, trying to swallow before she slowly stood up, looking frail but angry. "There is an assembly, mmm." It sounded as though each word was difficult to say but Sophie still smiled inwardly, pleased with their prediction. "Line up."

As usual, the children lined up one by one by the door. As they were doing so, Sophie took the opportunity to quickly and discreetly slip the salt into her pocket. She put the water pistol down the back of the waistband of her skirt, feeling like an American cop in the movies. She made her way to the door with the others and waited. Mrs French was already at the front of the line by the door, leaning against the wall. Her eyes were heavy and she looked weak. She gingerly stood away from where she had been resting and slowly led the class to the assembly.

Sophie grinned to herself and felt the adrenalin pumping through her body. She walked slowly and allowed the others to overtake her, until she was at the back of the line. As they made their way down the corridor, she pinned the orange badge to her uniform, making sure no one was looking, and slipped away from the rest of the group before making her way to Ms Malignus's office.

37.

Waiting in the hall, Ms Malignus watched as the children quietly entered. She made no attempt to disguise or hide the contempt and hate that she had for each of them. It was written across her face. They were all bland and unremarkable to her; each one the same, uninspired and ordinary. Their only use was the Sanguine that she was able to farm from them but that didn't matter now; all that mattered was finding those who had broken into her office and put everything at risk. She watched as the children entered the hall, studying their faces and looking for any sign of guilt or any indication of their wrongdoing. The Golems looked as passive as normal, each a perfect clone of their host, distinguishable only by their badges, but those she hadn't turned; those who were yet to be farmed, all looked the same. They were scared, she thought; they all feared her. This was to be expected but none of it was new. She scowled, full of venom as they tried to hide their faces from her. Today, she wouldn't let them.

Clack, clack, clack was the only sound in the hall as Ms Malignus walked amongst the children, her footsteps echoing off the walls. She studied each child as she passed them, taking some by the chin and lifting their heads up, looking for any hint of the guilt that they could be hiding. She turned and looked at the teachers, all of whom had taken their usual seats on the stage. All teachers' chairs were filled, except for the two spaces which belonged to Mr Dalty and Mrs Atchison, two of her more vicious and intimidating teachers, who were currently guarding her office, and the two that had belonged to Mr Parkes and Miss Betteridge.

Pathetic, dreadful, useless creatures, she thought as she surveyed them. She had denied them their Sanguine as a punishment for their failures last night and it showed as they sat, sloped and dazed in their chairs. They looked weak; half alive, even. She made a mental note to punish them further. The only two teachers who looked their normal selves were Mr Fields and Mrs Harper. She now hated them more than she hated any of the others. How dare they threaten her? How dare they try to position themselves as her equal? She cursed under her breath as she watched Mrs Harper writing notes in her book, recording everything; monitoring and observing her as if she had some power or authority.

Ms Malignus turned away from the teachers and stood at the front of the hall to look at the children in front of her. *Nothing*, she thought angrily as she watched their faces. There was no tell, no show or sign from any of them which might indicate who was responsible for last night's intrusion. *Vigilance and patience*, she growled to herself. *Eventually, they will show themselves to me.*

38.

Sophie made her way towards the main corridor and Ms Malignus's office. She, Ben, Jack and Lucy had arranged to meet there and enter the hidden passageway together. As she made her way along to the meeting place she tried to maintain the air of a prefect, walking as passively and devoid of expression as she could, making sure she was moving neither too fast nor too slow.

One or two of the teachers glanced at her as she made her way past their lines of children, who were going to the assembly hall, but none of them paid her too much attention. Sophie was amazed at how haggard and lethargic all of the teachers appeared but she did her best not to let this show on her face. When she finally reached the main corridor it was completely empty, with no sign of Lucy, Jack or Ben. She was already feeling anxious and nervous but this was made worse by their absence. She waited, growing more and more unsettled and afraid as the minutes ticked by. Worries and questions flooded her thoughts: What if something had happened to them? What if they weren't coming? She didn't think she could go through this and do what needed to be done alone. She paced backwards and forwards, watching out for any sign of them and wondering what she should do. Just as she was beginning to feel that something might have happened to them and they weren't going to make it, she saw Lucy finally turn the corner and enter the main corridor, closely followed by Jack. Relief flooded through Sophie when she saw her friends. Until she noticed the fear in their faces.

Jack looked at her, wide-eyed. "They've got Ben."

In the assembly hall, Malignus was becoming more and more frustrated. She stalked the rows of children, waiting, searching for a sign, for anything that would tell her who she was looking for, when suddenly the doors crashed open. She spun around to see Mr Dalty bursting through them, dragging a boy behind him. The boy was struggling hard and Mr Dalty was also struggling, to hold on to him, but despite this he was still grinning inanely. Ben's screams and shouts echoed around the hall. "I found him," Mr Dalty shouted above the din. "I found this one in the corridors, Headmistress."

"Quiet!" The headteacher screamed above Ben's cries. She rushed towards him and grabbed him by his red hair, stabbing her finger forcefully into his forehead. He immediately stopped struggling and became still in Mr Dalty's grasp. "Stand him up," she commanded as Mr Dalty held him out in front of her. She looked Ben up and down. At first there didn't seem to be anything out of the ordinary about him but then she noticed his orange badge. She didn't recognise this one. She looked at the children sitting in their rows. The whole hall was silent. Most of the children were looking at the floor or sitting with their eyes closed, too frightened to look up, whilst others were watching nervously, unable to turn away. She could pick out her Golems; she recognised all of them instantly, but not this one that had been caught. He hadn't been acting like they did, either; he had been screaming and shouting, not obedient like her others. She glanced over to the teachers, most of whom appeared withdrawn and sleepy, although some were grinning at her. Two, however, were talking between themselves. Rava Fields and Helena Harper were quietly whispering to each other. Fields was doing much more talking than Harper, whilst she was writing furiously in her book. Ms Malignus growled at the thought of them all. She turned back to Mr Dalty. "Where was he?" she snarled at him.

"Out in the corridor, by the girls' toilets," he answered, grinning, clearly pleased with his efforts.

She turned her attention back to Ben. "Who are you?" she whispered at him. "Where were you going, boy? To my office? Do you have it? You must have it?" She reached and felt his pockets, searching for her golden key. Her hideous guttural scream filled the hall when she found it wasn't there.

Jack and Lucy were talking over each other, both of them panicking and speaking as fast as they could, trying to get all of their words out at once. "It was Dalty," Jack gasped. "We were behind Ben, trying to catch him up."

"Ben hadn't seen us," Lucy interrupted.

"And it's good he hadn't or else Dalty would've done us as well," Jack blurted. "He just came out of nowhere, Soph."

"He just grabbed Ben and dragged him off," Lucy stammered.

"We couldn't stop it," Jack said, panicking. "Ben was shouting and screaming, his legs and arms were flying everywhere, trying to fight, but he just couldn't get Dalty off."

"We couldn't do anything. There were too many there," Lucy said. "Other teachers and kids."

"And the Watchouts, they were in the corridor as well," Jack added. "Going to the hall. We had to keep walking, like nothing had happened."

"We came straight here as fast as we could. I was terrified that you'd been got to," Lucy said, looking straight at Sophie. They were both flustered and upset.

Sophie shook her head. "We need to hurry," she said decisively, turning and looking down the corridor. All of her worries and doubts had now disappeared and she knew what she needed to do. "We need to do this quickly, before anything else happens." Without waiting for agreement or response from the others, she began to run along the corridor, heading towards the alcove outside Ms Malignus's office.

"Sophie, wait," Lucy hissed as she and Jack tried to catch up with her. They saw her disappear just ahead of them, as she raced into the alcove, then they heard her screaming wildly. They turned into the alcove to see Mrs Atchison blocking the office door and gripping Sophie tightly in her arms.

"No!" Jack screamed as he charged at the two of them. Sophie was fighting as hard as she could and was wriggling violently in Mrs Atchison's arms. He smashed into them both, sending them crashing through the office door. They landed in a heap, legs and arms all tangled together, with Mrs Atchison at the bottom of the pile, spit and phlegm flying from her mouth as she landed hard on her back and tried to fight back. Lucy rushed through the open door, slamming it shut behind her. Without thinking, she pulled out the water pistol filled with holy water and began firing it over the crumpled bodies. In spite of Jack's rush and the heavy fall to the floor, Mrs Atchison had managed to keep a grip on Sophie; however, the moment the water touched her skin, it began bubbling and melting and she screamed in agony. The teacher let go of the girl and tried to shield her face from the burning water with her arms but Lucy was relentless. Sophie and Jack managed to roll and crawl away from the screaming teacher but Lucy had stepped even closer and kept squirting the holy water until the pistol was empty. Mrs Atchison remained on the floor, rolling in pain, moaning as the water melted her skin. Lucy watched her for a moment before taking out the packet of salt and emptying the contents all over her. Mrs Atchison's scream rose in an almighty crescendo before quickly dying away as she dissolved under the salt. There was very soon nothing left but a pile of slime and gunk.

"Monsters not people," Lucy said quietly to herself.

39.

"Oh Lucy, thank you, thank you," Sophie cried as she threw her arms around her friend, hugging her tightly. Lucy closed her eyes and hugged back. "You were so brave," Sophie continued, "I don't know what would have happened if...?"

"Well, it didn't," Lucy said, answering the unasked question quietly and hugging Sophie hard, not letting go.

"Well done, Luce, that was pretty awesome," Jack said, grinning at her. Lucy smiled back at him and let go of Sophie.

"We haven't got time for this," she said abruptly, bringing herself back to why they were there in the first place. "We've got to get down to that cellar. Jack, do you still have those cricket stumps in your bag? I've got nothing left to defend myself with."

"Yeah," he answered, taking his bag off his shoulder and retrieving one of the stumps. It still had some of the slime that had once been Mr Parkes on it. He wiped it clean with his sleeve. "Only got the one, though, don't know where the other ended up," he said, smiling as he handed it to her. "You left this one at mine when you left last night." She blushed as she took it. "Oh," he said, suddenly remembering, "take this as well." He handed her the string of garlic.

She looked at him, confused. "They're for vampires, aren't they?"

"Well, you never know," he shrugged.

The three friends stood together in Malignus's office, silently reassuring each other and themselves. Jack looked at the bubbling, steaming pile of ooze, which used to be Mrs Atchison, pulsating in the middle of the room. "No backing out now," he said, turning his attention from it and looking at the large oak cupboard. He took hold of the door handle and looked up at the girls. Smiling, he pulled the door fully open in front of them, revealing the dark stairway. "I told you, no key needed." He laughed as he confidently stepped back from the door, showing them the way. "Ladies first," he said, winking and bowing down low.

"Stop messing about," Lucy said, punching him in the arm as she pushed past him. Sophie smiled kindly and followed her into the darkness, with Jack stepping through last. He paused as he watched the girls walk down the stairs and into the blackness below. Then he turned back and looked into the office gravely, before closing the door and following behind them.

They made their way down the stairs and into the passage, moving as quickly as they could in the dark. Lucy held her hands out in front of her, to feel her way forward. The journey felt longer this time and the passage more oppressive. She kept pushing on until she touched the warm, soft veil. "We're nearly there," she quietly called back to the other two. As she pushed through the veil, the foul smell of the passageway became more intense but despite this she continued to move forward until she reached the old wooden door.

She looked through the crack in the wood to make sure the cellar was empty. She couldn't see anyone, except for the lines of children, so she carefully pushed the door open. It creaked loudly; the sound echoing on the stone walls seemed deafening in the relative dark and quiet of the cellar. Behind her, she could hear Sophie gagging at the putrid smell that filled the room as both she and Jack followed her in.

In the dark and the gloom, they looked at the children standing in their rows. Lucy gasped, "There's so many of them. There's more than I thought there would be!"

"Are they dead?" Sophie asked tentatively. She had been so sure before that they weren't but now she doubted herself.

"No," Jack answered, looking closely at a young boy. "He's breathing, this one, only shallow, but he's definitely breathing."

"Look, there's Boz," Sophie called from across the cellar. She had been searching through the children and was holding her hand over her mouth and nose, trying to block out the smell of the room. They all went to where Boz stood sleeping lightly and looked him over.

Jack shook his head at the sight of his friend. "Why didn't you listen?" he quietly asked, placing his hand on his friend's chest. Although Boz was still breathing, he felt cold. Lucy touched Jack lightly on the shoulder and moved away. Jack sighed and followed her. They continued to search through the rows of children.

"Sophie, here's Tom," Lucy said, calling her over.

Sophie went to him and took his hand. "We'll save you, Tom," she whispered, hoping he could hear her. As she stood holding his hand she noticed something odd and began to look him up and down curiously, as if she was searching for something.

"This is awful," Lucy said, shocked at the rows of children lined up in front of her.

"What's that?" Jack asked, spotting something across the room. He made his way over to it through the gloom. "Look, there's that other door you mentioned, Lucy." He opened it and stepped through without waiting.

"Jack, no!" Lucy called as loudly as she dared. "That's the way French went." But he had already gone.

"Lucy!" Sophie called. She was still standing with Tom. "Come and look at this… Lucy." Lucy hadn't heard her and had already followed Jack out of the far door, leaving Sophie alone in the cellar with the children.

"Jack," Lucy hissed up the second passageway. Her voice echoed off the stone walls and chased after him. She stopped and listened to it, scared that someone or something other than Jack might answer. As she listened she noticed that it was also echoing to her side. She turned and saw the opening on her left, inside which were several bottles filled with a thick, brown liquid. They were easily the biggest bottles she had ever seen and she was sure that these were the same as the one that Mrs French had struggled to carry; the same ones that she had seen filled when Malignus 'milked' Tom. She wondered what they were. She was about to take one from the shelf to look at it more closely when she heard footsteps coming back down the passage. She froze and gripped the wooden cricket stump tightly, ready to strike whatever was coming towards her. She breathed a sigh of relief as she watched Jack run past her back into the cellar, completely oblivious to the fact she was there. She left the bottles and joined him and Sophie back in that horrible room.

"It's the staffroom," Jack said, gasping. He had run all the way up the passage and back again and was struggling to get his breath back in the stench of the room. "That way leads straight up to the staffroom," he stressed, "and it's empty, so we can get everyone out that way." He leaned forward and put his hands on his knees, breathing heavily.

"Ok," Sophie said quickly. "I've been looking at all of these and think I know how to release them." She walked over to one of the children. "They've all got these tubes and wires on them. Look." She showed them a young girl who was close to where they stood. There were small, thin tubes and wires attached to her stomach, arms and hands. They were barely visible. "I'd never have noticed them if I hadn't felt one on Tom's hand. Look, they've all got them." Jack and Lucy looked at the children. Now they knew what to look for, they could see the wires and tubes coming out of each child. Sophie showed them the gurneys that each child was attached to. "I think that if we untie them from these wooden bed things, and then release them from the tubes and wires, we can get them out." She waited for a response.

"Good work, Sophie, well spotted," Lucy replied, smiling at her. "It beats any ideas I had."

"Me too," Jack agreed, "It's better than anything I had." He took a deep breath to compose himself. "So, we get everyone unhooked and then help them out and up into the staffroom, and then out of the school." They all agreed. "Good, then let's do this."

One by one, they began to untie and free the children.

40.

*A*ll of the children and staff in the hall sat in stunned silence and stared in disbelief at Ms Malignus. Some of the children covered their ears, trying to hide from her hideous scream, whilst others sat open-mouthed, agog at the outburst from the headteacher, who had momentarily forgotten where she was, such was her turmoil at not finding the key. Even the teachers at the front of the hall, who were used to her wickedness and had seen her anger in the past, showed fear at her lack of control. All except for two. Mr Fields and Mrs Harper stopped whispering to each other and watched Ms Malignus carefully. Mrs Harper held her pen, hovering it above her notebook, momentarily pausing her writing. Both of them waited, unmoved, to see what she would do next.

Ms Malignus had forgotten about them, and everyone else that was in the hall. All she cared about at that moment was her key and she was now, for the first time, beginning to panic. If this boy didn't have it then someone else must. Which must mean that there are more people who knew about their secrets, but who were they, and where were they? She began to shake Ben violently. "Where is it?" she screamed at him, "Who has it?" Ben remained passive, not moving or resisting her in any way, completely unable to tell her anything, even if he had wanted to. Malignus threw him to the floor in anger. She was furious with herself for quietening him earlier when he was screaming and shouting as it now meant that he couldn't give her any of the information she'd wanted. When she had silenced him she had been certain that she was about to retrieve her key. How could she have known there were others? She stared at the boy on the floor, her mind racing with possible dangers and threats. She froze, realising that the danger to her school was growing. She grabbed Mr Dalty.

"There are more," she growled; "others in the school. Find them, find them all."

It was then that she noticed something happening. In that moment of clarity, when she felt vulnerable and threatened, she noticed something unusual happening to the children who were sitting watching.

"Quick, this way," Lucy called, hurrying the children they had managed to release over to where she was waiting, at the far end of the cellar. They had agreed that she was to help the ones they had freed, whilst Jack and Sophie were to continue working their way along the rows of children, releasing them from their gurneys and from the tubes and wires which had, up until this point, been keeping them alive. The whole process was taking longer than they had wanted, however, and Lucy was beginning to grow anxious. The longer they were there, the more likely it was that they would get caught. She willed them all to hurry up. Each child they released was weak and confused, especially those that had been imprisoned in the cellar for the longest. Each needed to be helped over to Lucy as they couldn't yet walk steadily for themselves. None of them knew where they were, or how they'd got there, and they were all upset and disorientated. It was Lucy's job to help them remain calm and try to focus them, getting them back on their feet and making sure they were ready to move.

Sophie paused when she came to release Tom. Taking as much care as she could she gently pulled the wire from his hand. She then removed the tubes that had been feeding him and released the straps that had been holding him to the gurney. She took his weight as he fell against her and held him tight. Holding him close she whispered, "Tom, Tom, you need to wake up. You need to stand." Slowly, he shook his head, trying to bring himself around. It was difficult to focus in the darkness of the cellar but gradually the vague shapes began to take form.

"Sophie?" he whispered, his voice cracked and sore. "Sophie, is that you?" He tried to stand on his own, leaning into her for the support that he needed. At first he was unsteady but she was able to take his weight. Gradually, his balance began to return. "Sophie, what's happening? Where am I?" he asked, confused and scared.

"Shh," she whispered, "not now. I'll tell you everything in a bit, but now we have to hurry." She put his arm around her to support him and helped him over to where Lucy was waiting. She was quietly talking to some of the other children they had released.

"How much longer?" she asked when she saw Sophie approaching.

"Not many now, nearly done." Sophie handed Tom over to her. "Tom, wait here with Lucy, I've got to go and help the others." Lucy took hold of Tom and led him across to where another boy was leaning against the cellar wall. She watched Sophie run back to free the last few children.

Ms Malignus had blocked out and ignored all of the sounds coming from the children in the hall. Their crying and snivelling had only served as distractions against her finding her key but they had her attention now. Now, their noises were different, and something strange was happening, but what was it? She looked across the hall. Several of them were in tears, crying like babies, but it wasn't because of her. They weren't even looking at her but at the spaces in their rows. Something was nagging away at her, in the back of her mind, but she couldn't quite place what it was. The cries and sobbing from the children grew louder, some were screaming. *Spaces*, she thought. What was it about the spaces that was nagging away at her? Then she realised. It was the spaces themselves. They shouldn't be there. *They weren't there before*, she thought, *so where did they come from?* Slowly, she walked towards one, a nervousness that she had never felt before growing over her.

She looked at the space to see a pile of clay had spilt across the chair and onto the floor. A small orange badge was lying next to it. As she looked across the hall she noticed more and more piles of clay, where once there had been pupils. "Not just any pupils," she whispered to herself, "no, they were my pupils. My Golems." Just then, a prefect sitting next to her began to shake. The shaking grew faster and faster, becoming more and more vigorous, until the body simply crumbled away, leaving nothing but clay on the seat and floor, the orange badge falling into it. Fear and panic flooded her body as she realised what was happening. Someone must be in her cellar, releasing and unhooking the Golem hosts. She looked over to Mr Fields and Mrs Harper. Fields had also seen what was happening and had come to the same realisation. He was furious, his face red with anger, as he watched his precious Golems returning to the clay from which he had shaped them. Harper, meanwhile, was writing furiously in her notebook, shaking her head, recording the events for the reports she would send to the Academy directors.

"No, no, no," Malignus shouted as she watched them both stand up and walk out of the hall. "This can't be…"

She began to run, pushing chairs and children out of her way as she rushed toward the hall doors, needing to get to her office and the cellar. She had to stop this. "Now, with me, all of you," she screamed at the teachers as she ran. "Follow me." Slowly, and with huge effort, they rose from their chairs and began to follow her, leaving the remaining children alone in the hall.

41.

*B*en lay on the floor and listened to the sounds around him. All he could hear was the commotion of children screaming and crying, as if the whole hall was in turmoil and chaos was all around. He unsuccessfully tried to move but he was in pain and was aching all over his body, his head throbbing, leaving him feeling like he'd been hit with a sledgehammer. His memory was a bit hazy and it felt as though he was looking through thick fog as he tried to recall what had happened. He remembered making his way towards the main corridor to meet the others; the corridor he was in was full of people, though, and he couldn't get out of it. That's when he was hit; grabbed from behind by someone. He wasn't sure who it was but they stank and were tall... really, really tall. It must have been Dalty, he thought, but he couldn't be totally sure. He'd tried to fight them off, but he'd dropped his bag with all of his weapons and couldn't get free. Whoever it was, they were really strong and just would not let him go. The next thing he remembered was being in the hall. Malignus was there. Then there was nothing. Just a white light and sleepiness. There were some vague noises and shouts but they felt like a dream; nothing was real; nothing that he could call solid or concrete.

As he lay on the floor, his focus slowly began to return to him. Unsteadily, he sat up and looked around. He was still in the hall, he knew that much, and knew that it was a good thing but he could tell that something was different, something was wrong. There were children all around him, crying; people he knew, his mates, in tears and upset. Clumsily, he got to his feet. He couldn't see any teachers. There were no teachers anywhere. Only children.

All of a sudden, he felt someone crash into him as their arms wrapped around him, tightly squeezing.

"Oh my God, Ben, are you ok?" Charlie cried as she hugged him. "I couldn't believe it was you when Dalty dragged you in." He pushed her away from him.

"Charlie," he quickly said, "what's going on here? What's happened?"

She looked at him, confused. "What do you mean? You were here the whole time."

He shook his head. "Charlie, I feel like I've been hit by a bus. Everything is a blur. Please, just tell me what happened? Why is everyone so upset? Where are the teachers?"

She quickly told him everything that had gone on during the assembly. From Malignus screaming at him, to the prefects all just starting to disappear, and how Malignus and the rest of the teachers had run out of the hall. Ben listened until he realised where they had all gone. "Jack," he suddenly said. "That's where they're going. They're going to the cellar to stop him." He turned to run but Charlie grabbed his arm.

"Ben, what's happened?" she asked tentatively.

"It's all true, Charlie," he said, looking her straight in the face. "Everything Jack said about the cellar and those Golem things. It's all true. I've got to go and help them." She held on to his arm and wouldn't let it go. He pulled away.

"Ben," she said, looking worried. "I don't know what's going on but you're scaring me." He turned and looked at her, wanting to get away.

"Just believe me, Charlie, it's true; all of it. They're all monsters here." He stopped trying to get away and looked around the hall, at the children scared and crying. A new thought crossed his mind. "We've got to get them out." He felt torn. He knew that he had to go and help Jack and the girls, and that every wasted second counted against them, but he also knew that he could help every single person in that hall just by simply getting them out of the school. The options flew around his head until he made his decision. "Listen," he said to his friend, "don't ask, I'll explain everything better later but everyone here, now, in this hall, is in danger. We've got to get them out."

"Are you serious?" she asked nervously.

"Never more so," he answered, "go and get the others, we'll need their help." He ran to the stage, where the teachers usually sat, and jumped up on it. The hall was alive with children talking and crying. Looking out across it, he could see how upset and scared everyone was. He put two fingers into his mouth and blew the loudest whistle he could. Instantly, the hall fell silent, as everyone turned to look at him. "Listen, everyone," he shouted as loudly as he could. "You've all seen what has happened. You've all seen what this place is, and you all know that it isn't normal. Well, you're right. It isn't, and none of us is safe here." He paused for a moment, letting his words sink in and making sure he had the attention of all of them. He could see Charlie waiting by the door Mr Dalty had dragged him through. "We're all in danger if we stay here," he continued, "and we've got to get out." Harry was now standing next to Charlie, both of them ready to go. "Everyone, follow Charlie and get out. Now."

Quickly, the children started to do what he had said. Kate, Claire and some of the other older children began martialling the younger ones to the doors, where Charlie and Harry were waiting. He watched as they left the hall, following Charlie and Harry out to safety. Only when the last child had left did Ben himself go. Jumping off the stage, he ran as fast as he could to the cellar, to help Jack and the others.

42.

Jack carefully released Boz and helped him down from the gurney. He put his arms around him. "Take it easy, mate," he said, supporting him as they made their way to the far end of the cellar. "Come on, nearly there." Encouraging him to walk faster so they could get out as quickly as possible. "This is the last one," he shouted to Sophie and Lucy as he approached them, "let's go."

Lucy held open the old wooden door. "Sophie, you go first," she said, "lead the way up to the staffroom. I'll follow you with Jack. We've got to get everyone outside and away from the school."

Sophie nodded and took hold of Tom's hand. "You need to help me get everyone out," she said, leading him to the door. He was still in shock and shivering but nodded his head in agreement, accepting her hand and going along with her. Together, they encouraged the other children to leave the cellar and make their way along the cold, dark passageway to the staffroom. Like Tom, many of them were still in a state of shock; they were dirty, cold, and they were frightened. Only just awoken from a deep, dark dream, they needed plenty of encouragement to stumble forward into the darkness.

"Come on, come on," Lucy repeated, trying to hurry the children through the door. She looked at Jack. Boz wasn't leaning on him as much now and seemed to be supporting himself more as he slowly shuffled towards her. As the children passed, making their way to the staffroom, she began to think about the cellar and everything that had been going on, right under their noses. She thought of why they were there and why the teachers needed the children. She then remembered the bottle she had seen Mrs French filling and the other huge bottles that she had seen stored in that small opening. She had been right next to it but up until that moment had completely forgotten it was there. Leaving the children to follow each other and make their way up the passageway, she went back to have another look. She stared at the rows of full bottles, each containing the same red, copper-brown liquid, and took one down to look at it more closely, struggling under its weight. She swirled the bottle in her hands and watched as the contents spun inside, the thick liquid glooping and swooshing about. She was mesmerised and kept swilling it backwards and forwards. It seemed to shine and shimmer ever so slightly in the darkness. She carried it back to the open door. "Jack," she called, "what do you think this stuff is? It's what French was... Jack, look out!"

Before she could finish her sentence she saw the long, tall, spindly figure of Ms Malignus appear in the doorway behind him. Lucy screamed as Jack spun around. Seeing Malignus rushing at him, he pushed Boz towards Lucy. "Run!" he shouted at them both as he scrambled to try and get his backpack from his shoulders. Malignus shrieked in rage and horror as she saw her empty cellar. She ran straight at Jack, full of fury, and hit him hard in the head, knocking him straight to the floor. She stopped and stood over his motionless body, glaring at him, full of hate and anger.

"Jack!" Lucy screamed. Malignus tore her attention away from the prone boy and looked up in the direction of the scream, just in time to see Boz staggering through the door.

"No," she growled under her breath. She suddenly noticed Lucy, as well; holding the bottle of Sanguine. Malignus stopped abruptly and stared at the girl, full of venom. "How dare you, child? Put that down. Now."

"Stay where you are," Lucy shouted, terrified by the monster standing in front of her. Boz waited behind her, exhausted and leaning against the wall. "Jack!" Lucy called again. Malignus's eyes never left the bottle she was holding.

"*Jack*," Malignus mocked, her voice high and chilling. She smirked at Lucy and began slowly inching forward.

"Stay there," Lucy screamed. She held the huge bottle up as high as she could. Malignus froze, not willing to risk Lucy dropping the precious liquid. "Jack… please…" Lucy begged, tears starting to build in her eyes as she willed him to get up or even just to move. But he didn't. Nothing happened. He lay, motionless, on the floor, where he had landed after Malignus had struck him.

"He can't hear you now, little girl," Malignus cackled, her voice dripping with malice. "Not now." She laughed. She leaned forward and held her hand out, "Now give me the bottle and I'll let you live." Lucy looked at Jack, lying on the dirty cellar floor. She sniffed, letting her tears fall for her dead friend. She thought of him saving her and how close they had become, and looked back at Malignus with hatred. How could she have taken him away from her? How could she stand there laughing and smiling about it? How could he be dead?

"You can have your stupid bottle," she yelled, and with great effort threw it as far as she could across the cellar before grabbing Boz and running as quickly as possible, back along the passageway towards the exit in the staffroom. Malignus screamed as the huge bottle flew through the air. She launched herself at it, trying to catch it, but she was too slow. It smashed into pieces as it struck the cold, hard floor. Glass splintered all over the ground and the reddish-brown liquid slowly began to form a thick puddle around the pieces. Malignus fell to her knees, trying to scoop up the precious Sanguine, howling in anguish as she did so, momentarily forgetting about the escaping children.

43.

Lucy and Boz quickly staggered up the passageway. He was still unsteady on his feet but she pushed him to move as quickly as he could. They had only gone a short distance when Lucy stopped. "Boz, you've got to keep going, get out and tell someone what's been happening here," she told him, breathing heavily after their exertions. "When you get to the staffroom, make sure you barricade the door. Nothing can get out of here, do you understand? I can't leave Jack's body to them."

"No chance," Boz replied quickly. He too was out of breath, leaning heavily against the wall, "there's no way you're going back down there."

"I've got to get him," Lucy argued.

"Fine, then I'll come too," Boz argued back. "I've already turned away from him once. I'm not doing it again."

"Look at you," Lucy protested angrily. "You can barely stand as it is. You're too weak and wouldn't be able to do anything. Just please do as I say and go, and make sure nothing can get out of this tunnel. I've got a plan; I'll take Jack out the other way, through her office." Boz began to argue again but she stopped him in his tracks and held the wooden cricket stump tightly in front of her. "Now isn't the time, Boz. Just go!"

He stared at her angrily but could see the determination on her face. He also knew she was right; he was far too weak and would be more of a burden than a help. After much soul-searching, he eventually agreed.

Lucy watched as he reluctantly began to make his way along the passage, holding the wall for support. She let out a deep breath. She had lied to him and had no idea what she was going to do, but knew she had to do something. Resolutely, she quietly began to make her way back to the cellar.

In her desire to save her precious Sanguine, Malignus had forgotten all about Lucy and Boz escaping. She was on her knees, surrounded by the thick spilled liquid, lost in furious thoughts at how important each drop was for the Academy and how this waste, this disaster, could harm her ambitions, when she heard a shuffling noise. She looked up from the thick, congealed mess on the floor to see that slowly, one by one, her teachers were creeping into the cellar. They had all been in the assembly and had all followed her here. Most of them had never been in her cellar and were cautiously looking around at their surroundings. Mr Dalty had been the first to enter, followed by Mrs French, who knew all about this place and what was kept here, with the remaining staff in the school following behind them. Mrs French was looking at Jack lying lifeless on the floor but Mr Dalty's eyes were locked straight on Malignus. He slowly lowered his gaze and spotted the copper-brown liquid she was kneeling in. Realising what it was, he greedily homed in on it as it oozed across the floor. He grinned ravenously as he inched his way slowly towards her. Mrs French had also noticed the spilt liquid, as had most of the other teachers. "Mmm, mmm," she murmured in her hunger, her tongue flicking in and out of her mouth, tasting the air as they all moved closer and closer to the spilt Sanguine.

"Get away, all of you!" Malignus commanded as they crept nearer, fear starting to show in her voice. She tried to get to her feet but slipped in the liquid. "I order you, stay away!" But the teachers weren't listening. They had been starved and were weak. Their only thought was the feed that Malignus was scrambling in.

Mr Dalty dived on top of her, pushing her to the floor as he desperately scrambled to reach the Sanguine. Mrs French and the other teachers immediately followed, each desperate to appease their starved appetites. They clawed and pulled at one another, trying to suck up the liquid from the floor; scratching, hitting, biting and pushing each other, oblivious to the broken glass which cut their mouths and tongues, all in their need for the spilt Sanguine which had been denied to them. Ms Malignus was now no longer their headteacher but just another body in their way; just someone they had to fight and compete against, and she was being crushed under the weight of the frenetic scramble. Her screams and cries lost in the mad crush.

Lucy quietly crept back towards the cellar. The garlic string was hanging from her neck and the wooden cricket stump was held tightly, ready to stab at anything that she might meet. She was surprised to find no resistance but could hear strange noises echoing up the passageway, which became louder the closer she got to the door. When she reached it she pressed her face against it and listened. She could hear growls and grunts and strange scuffling noises. Opening the door fractionally to look inside, she was astonished to see the teachers rolling on the floor, fighting and climbing over each other. She looked closer, to try and see what they were fighting over, and was surprised to see them licking the ground, grabbing and climbing all over each other for the thick liquid that had been in the huge bottle she had thrown.

This gave her an idea.

She returned to the opening and retrieved another bottle of the brown liquid. Taking a deep breath, she opened the door and went back into the cellar to retrieve Jack's body.

Quietly and carefully, she inched her way across the cellar, heading towards his prone body, desperate not to be noticed by anyone. She watched in disgust as the monsters writhed and fought each other, greedily trying to lap up as much of the liquid as they could. They no longer appeared to be remotely teacher-like, or human in any way, but instead were like great monstrous insects, clambering over each other to get to their food. Thankful that they weren't interested in her and that she couldn't see any sign of Malignus, Lucy continued trying to reach Jack. However, just as she was almost close enough to grab him, she stopped and froze. Dalty was perched on his heels, crouched motionless in front of her but grinning inanely. He was staring intently at the bottle she was carrying. Slowly and very deliberately, she held it out in front of him and started swinging it to and fro. His eyes never left it as he copied the swinging motion with his head, hypnotised and intoxicated by the special liquid. She swung the bottle a few more times before throwing it across the room. He dived after it, hungrily followed by more of the teachers.

Lucy quickly fell to her knees in front of Jack's body. "Oh, Jack," she murmured softly, letting her tears fall on him. She wanted to stay longer, to hold him and mourn him, but she knew she couldn't. She had to get them both out quickly. She put the cricket stump on the floor next to him and, using both hands, took his arm. She was about to try and lift him onto her shoulder when she felt a cold, claw-like hand clasp tightly around her neck. She instinctively dropped Jack's arm and grabbed at the claw, trying to loosen its grip, but it was too strong. Lucy coughed and spluttered, slowly being choked as the claw tightened its grasp and lifted her into the air, pushing her up against the wall. Hanging there, desperately trying to release herself, she looked to see that it was Ms Malignus who was slowly strangling her. The headteacher's face was bruised and bloody, her clothes were ripped, and there was dirt smeared all over her. He hair had been torn out of its usual neat, tight bob, and she was snarling like a wild animal at Lucy.

"You will suffer for this," she spat, sputum and spittle flying everywhere. "You have ruined everything." Lucy was choking, Malignus's grip getting tighter and tighter around her throat. She kicked and squirmed but could not break free. She clawed at Malignus's hands and reached into her face, scratching it, but Malignus would not let go. Lucy grabbed at the string of garlic that was hanging around her neck and in a final attempt at freedom thrust it into Malignus's evil face. She swatted it away. "Garlic doesn't work, little girl," she laughed.

"No, but I bet fire does!" A voice shouted out as a ball of flame engulfed Malignus, who roared in agony, dropping Lucy to the floor. Lucy turned to see Jack spraying fire-bursts at the monster in front of him. Malignus screamed as flames spewed from the deodorant can, catching on her clothes and spreading all over her body. Jack was relentless, the home-made flame-thrower setting fire to every part of her. Malignus reached out to grab him but erupted in agony as Lucy, who had moved quickly to help, stabbed her from behind with the wooden cricket stump, which she had left by Jack's inert body but had now managed to retrieve. Malignus stopped, the wooden stake thrust through her chest as the flames around her grew higher and higher. She gave out a blood-curdling scream before exploding violently, sending flames and fireballs across the cellar and covering Jack and Lucy in pus and ooze.

The fire began to spread. The wooden gurneys began to burn brightly and even the Sanguine began to burst into flames. Lucy threw her arms around Jack, "Jack, you're alive... I thought she'd... I thought you were..." Unable to say the words, she just hugged him tightly. He hugged her back and for the briefest moment the two of them forgot where they were and the danger they were in, both just happy to be with the other.

"We've got to go," Lucy said. "We can't stay here."

"You're right," Jack coughed in the smoke, which was beginning to fill the room. They stopped hugging each other.

"This way," Lucy yelled, taking his hand and leading him through the door and into the passageway that led to Malignus's office. The flames were building as the fire began to spread and they staggered through the smoke, coughing and spluttering. Just as they were stepping through the wooden door, a wild howl ran through the cellar. Jack stopped and turned around, to see where it had come from. Several of the monsters were covered in flames, howling and screaming, rolling around on the floor. As they lurched and writhed in pain, the flammable liquid around them ignited. Other monsters, still fighting to get to the liquid, were oblivious to the flames and soon became engulfed in the inferno themselves.

"Lucy, run!" Jack shouted, pushing her through the door and into the passage beyond. They sprinted as fast as they could as the tunnel began to fill with thick, black smoke creeping up from the cellar below. Spluttering, they ran up the stone steps and burst through the oak cupboard doors, back into Malignus's office, falling onto the floor and straight into the gloopy puddle that had been Mrs Atchison. Jack sat up and looked back through the open doors at the smoke. He quickly jumped up and slammed the doors shut, locking them with the small golden key.

44.

"Jack… Lucy… What?" Ben stuttered as he rushed into the office. Jack was slumped up against the doors of the now locked, large oak cupboard and Lucy was still on the floor, pushing herself slowly and wearily out of the gloopy puddle she had landed in. Thin wisps of black smoke were starting to seep through the gaps in the cupboard door. Jack was still gasping, trying to get his breath back, whilst Lucy coughed and spluttered on the floor.

"Fire… down there… got to run!" Jack coughed, in between long breaths. "Down… in the… in the… cellar." Ben immediately rushed to Lucy and helped her up from the floor.

"Quickly," he said, taking her hand and pulling her to her feet. They followed Ben into the alcove and the main corridor but Jack turned and ran back into Malignus's office. Thick, black smoke was now billowing into the room, through the cupboard, from the inferno below. Jack grabbed the small golden key from its lock and ran out of the room, closing the door behind him.

The fire below was raging and spreading throughout the cellar. The bottles containing the Sanguine began to bubble as the heat and inferno spread into the store room. As the liquid inside began to boil, the glass bottles shattered and the flammable liquid sprayed everywhere, causing the store room to explode.

"What was that?" Ben screamed as the school shook on its foundations with the force of the explosion.

"Don't care, just run," Jack shouted, determined that they would make their escape. Ben smashed the first fire alarm he saw with his fist, without breaking his stride.

"Where is everyone?" Lucy yelled at him as they ran along the corridor.

"All the kids are outside, all the teachers followed Malignus. I don't know where she was going, though," he answered above the din of the fire alarms.

"She was in the cellar," Lucy shouted, "with the rest of the teachers. I'll fill you in properly when we get out of here." Ben nodded and the three of them continued to run down the deserted corridors, and finally out of the school.

Charlie, Harry and the others had followed Ben's instructions and led all of the children out of the school. Malignus's stranger-than-normal behaviour during the assembly; the disappearing prefects, who had now reappeared on the field covered in filth and grime; and the fire alarms echoing around the grounds had left many of them shocked and confused. The rumble of the explosion in the cellar had only added to the fear, dread and anxiety many of them were experiencing, and groups of tearful children could be seen comforting and helping each other. All of them were gathered on the field at the back of the school, sitting in small groups on the grass or looking at the building, wondering what was going on. Funnily, other than the sounds of the alarms ringing loudly, the school showed very little sign of the fire that was raging below it. Jack, Lucy and Ben wandered across the fields, catching their breath and filling their lungs with fresh air, until they found Boz, who was sitting with Katie, Harry, Charlie and Claire. They made their way over to join them.

"Lucy, I was so scared," Boz said when he saw her. "I was terrified you wouldn't get out." His voice sounded strange, wobbly and unnatural. His eyes were half closed, and he appeared vacant. He shook his head as if he was struggling to maintain his thoughts. "Did you get him?"

"I did," she smiled.

"Jack!" Boz said, looking shocked to see him alive, but also pleased. "I thought you…" His voice trailed away, like he had forgotten to finish what he was saying.

"Well, I'm glad to say I'm not," Jack replied, slightly concerned by his unusual behaviour. "Are you alright?" Boz didn't answer but looked at Jack as if he couldn't focus on him properly.

"Where's Sophie?" Lucy asked, looking around for her friend and not picking up on Boz's strange behaviour.

"You two sit down and rest," Ben said, noticing how exhausted she and Jack both looked. "I'll go and find her." Lucy was about to argue with him; she desperately wanted to make sure Sophie was safe and wanted them all to look together, but Jack stopped her.

"Luce, I could really do with sitting down for a bit," he said, flopping down on the grass, slightly away from the others. "Besides, I'm sure she'll be ok and Ben will find her. Stay with me?" He held his hand out. She reluctantly took it and sat down next to him, though she continually looked around for any sign of Sophie.

It was the hot spring day that it had earlier promised to be and there wasn't a cloud in the sky. Jack lay on the grass with his head on her lap and felt the sun shining down on him whilst Lucy absently played with his hair. "Guys, I erm, I'm sorry," Boz said, coming over and sitting down next to them. "For not believing in you."

"You should be sorry," Jack answered without opening his eyes, "but I wouldn't worry about it now." He opened one eye and looked at Boz, who was swaying slightly and rubbing his temples. He looked as though he had a headache. "What was it like, Boz?" Jack asked cautiously, not wanting to upset him.

Boz started to rub his temples with his fingers and looked at the floor. "It was strange," he answered, looking as though he was straining to concentrate. "It's hard to recall but it was like being in a dream; you could see yourself doing things but you couldn't control any of it." He shook his head again and closed his eyes. "Bit like being a passenger when someone is driving."

"Do you remember anything about the cellar, or what they were doing to you?" Lucy asked.

"What?" Boz looked at her strangely, like he was seeing her for the first time. "No, no nothing… but you were there. Both of you… you were there and you left… no, I left." He shook his head again and closed his eyes, rubbing them with his hands. Lucy looked at him curiously. "It's vague," he said. "It's hard to remember."

Jack looked at Lucy with an expression of confusion and concern over Boz's strange behaviour.

"So you know what your Golem was doing but not you?" she pressed, wanting to know exactly what he could recall.

"Golem?" He looked confused, "What…? I mean, yeah… sort of. Like I said, it's fuzzy."

A voice shouted out, "Lucy!"

Her attention drawn away from Boz, Lucy looked up, searching for the source of the shout. "Sophie!" she shouted, seeing her friend. She waved at her wildly and quickly jumped to her feet, pushing Jack's head off her lap. Ben had found Sophie talking with Tom and they were all walking towards the group. Sophie had been equally as keen as Lucy had been to find her friend and she ran over as soon as she saw her, grabbing her and leaving the two boys to follow behind. The two girls hugged each other tightly. "I'm so glad to see you," Lucy whispered.

"You, too," Sophie replied. "I was so worried."

"Did everyone get out, Sophie?" Jack asked, serious again.

"Yeah," she said, smiling. "All of them got out but it was really strange."

"What do you mean?"

"Well, when we got away, we ran, trying to get out of the school, and we saw everyone else leaving as well, so we ended up getting mixed in with them. But after a short while they started acting a bit strange. Even Tom. People had gone off with their own mates and other than them being filthy, it was like nothing had happened."

"What's happened?" Boz asked, standing beside Jack. He had stopped shaking his head and his eyes looked clear and bright; apart from the dirt on his uniform, he looked just like his normal, usual self.

Jack turned to look at him. "What do you mean?" he asked, confused.

"Exactly what I said," Boz replied, glaring at him. "What's happened? Do you know why Malignus ran off and why Ben told everyone to leave?" Boz asked seriously. Jack looked at him, dumbfounded.

"See what I mean?" Sophie whispered. "Boz, what's the last thing you can remember?"

He looked at her strangely. "The assembly, then here." He laughed.

"What about the cellar?" Lucy quickly asked, becoming equally confused by his replies.

"What cellar?"

"We were talking about it just now," Jack snapped.

"I don't know what you're going on about, Jack," Boz said, shaking his head and growing reluctant to continue the conversation. He turned away and went back to where the girls were sitting. Jack watched him before turning to Sophie.

"What?" he shrugged.

"They're all the same, Jack," she sighed, "even Tom. Look." Ben and Tom had just caught them up. She turned to Tom. "Where have you just been, Tom?"

"We've just talked about this, Sophie," he answered, fed up. He was wiping the dirt off his uniform as he spoke. "You know where I was."

"Just tell me again," she requested.

"Assembly, and then here with you." He huffed. She smiled at him then turned back to Jack. "They don't remember anything," she said, looking sad and watching Tom as he lay down on the grass and closed his eyes. "He doesn't even remember going into her office. He can't remember the cellar, or assembly, or anything."

"You said Malignus had him all afternoon, didn't you, before his Golem appeared?" Lucy asked. Sophie nodded in agreement. "Maybe she had him that long because she had to make him forget it all?"

Sophie shrugged. "Could be. Who knows? But they don't remember any of it. None of them."

The sounds of fire engines could be heard in the distance, gradually getting louder.

"You mean we're the only ones who know?" Jack asked quietly.

"Looks like it," Sophie replied softly.

"It must be the Golems, or whatever they do to make them," Lucy interrupted. "Think about it, Boz said everything was like a dream but he knew what his Golem had been doing."

"Tom said something similar, before he started forgetting it all," Sophie said. "He said it felt like he was a passenger."

Lucy nodded, becoming animated. "Then they slowly forget everything," she snipped angrily. "Everything about the cellar, or Malignus. All of it is forgotten and then the Golem's memories become theirs and they just carry on as normal, like nothing has happened to them."

"My head hurts. That's way too much to think about," Jack said, sitting back down on the floor. "So we're the only ones who know any of it?"

"Could well be," Lucy sighed, sitting down next to him.

"We're not the only ones," Ben said assertively, pointing to the other side of the school field. "Look over there." The fire engines had entered the school via the iron gates. One of them had made its way to the back of the school, and several firefighters could be seen walking around. Many of the children were straining their necks to get a better view. Lucy looked over to where Ben was pointing and saw three figures talking to the chief firefighter, one of whom was holding a clipboard.

"Harper, Fields and Thomass," she said through gritted teeth, staring at the teachers in the distance.

"I knew Thomass wouldn't make it to the assembly," Jack said, chuckling to himself and lying down with his hands behind his head, too tired to look up. "The fat old slug never leaves that office!"

45.

The sun beat down on Jack as he lay daydreaming on the school field. It was a glorious day and he oddly felt completely at peace as he lay on the grass, holding Lucy's hand. He had stopped thinking about what had happened in the cellar and was simply enjoying that peaceful moment. Lucy was next to him, talking with Sophie, but he wasn't listening. At that moment, he didn't care about anything they were saying. *I'm done*, he thought to himself. *Everything else can wait until tomorrow.*

After a short while, he felt Lucy jabbing him in the ribs. "Jack, wake up. Harper is coming." Instantly, all of the horrors came flooding back to him. The monstrous teachers; the cellar; the fire; Malignus; all the thoughts he had pushed away came streaming back into his consciousness as he was jolted to reality. He sat up quickly and saw the small librarian heading in their direction. She was talking to groups of children as she passed them. Jack felt all of his muscles tense up as she drew near but tried hard not to show it. He felt Lucy's grip tighten in his hand and wished he hadn't left his backpack down in the cellar.

"Hello," Mrs Harper smiled as she reached them. No one smiled back at her but she didn't seem to notice. "As I'm sure you're no doubt aware, there has been an incident in the school." Ben turned away from her, hoping not to be noticed.

Sophie looked at her, concerned. "What's happened Miss?"

"Well, we don't really know any of the full details yet," Mrs Harper smiled, trying to reassure her. She had obviously been asked the same question several times as she spoke to the student groups. "But we do know there has been a fire."

Sophie tried to look shocked. "I thought the alarms were just a fire drill."

"Has anybody been hurt, Miss?" Lucy asked. Like Sophie, she had realised that if they seemed genuine and concerned and asked relevant questions then they would appear more normal. After all, if they hadn't been involved they wouldn't know what had happened.

Mrs Harper looked at her sympathetically. "Fortunately, the Fire Chief has said the fire was contained in a small part of the school but unfortunately we don't know if there has been any damage or any injuries yet." She looked at them all sadly, well-practised in the news she was giving. "But please don't worry, we will know more soon. For now, everyone is being sent home whilst they put out the last of the fire and the Fire Chief carries out her investigations." She smiled at them. "Your parents will be told what has happened and will be informed when it is safe to return to school and please make sure you sign out with Miss Thomass, who will be waiting at the main gates, before you leave." She waited, smiling at them for a moment, in case they had any further questions, before moving over to another group of pupils and giving them the same news.

"Back to mine, then?" Jack asked. "My mom's in but she won't mind as long as we keep the noise down."

They all agreed and slowly began to move, walking across the fields round the side of the school, ambling in the sun to the front of the building.

"What do you think will happen next?" Lucy asked Sophie, looking up at the large school as she walked past. Jack, Ben and Tom were walking just ahead of the two girls. Boz and the others had long gone.

"I don't know," Sophie answered, "but all of those monsters have gone, haven't they?"

"They must be gone," Lucy replied. "I can't see how they could have got out of that cellar. The fire was huge and they were all right in the middle of it." She stopped speaking abruptly, not wanting or ready to relive that moment in the cellar. Sophie didn't ask anything else.

They quietly walked across the school yard and under the stone archway, onto the long drive. "You and Jack look close," Sophie said, smiling. Lucy smiled back and looked happy; it was good to be thinking about something nice after the day she'd had.

"Yeah, I think we are," she grinned. "What about you and Tom?"

Sophie sighed. "I don't know. I like him but I don't think he's keen."

Lucy nudged her in the side. "Give him time, boys are idiots."

They laughed together and linked arms as they approached the large, iron gates, where Miss Thomass stood, holding several clipboards. She looked awful, as though her whole world had been taken from her, and that school was the last place she wanted to be. "Sssign againsst your name," she mumbled quietly, not looking up at any of the children but simply handing them the registers. They all signed themselves out of school and slowly strolled to Jack's house.

46.

The school was closed so that the fire could be investigated properly, leaving Sophie, Lucy, Jack and Ben plenty of time to go through everything that had happened. Spring quickly turned into summer and during the school closure the four spent most of their spare time with each other. They often met up at one or another's house, or just found a quiet place, like one of the local parks or wooded areas, where they could sit together in privacy and chat. Ben had suggested they climb over the school wall again and hang out in the Den, as no one would be there. He even went as far to suggest they break into the school to see what had happened to Malignus and the others but nobody else thought this a good idea. They wanted to stay as far away from the place as they could. They did, however, all feel that they didn't want to be left alone, privately dwelling and rerunning everything that they had been through. They much preferred to try and piece together the little bits of information they each had, and try to build as complete a picture as they could. Ben's account of what had happened during the final assembly was pretty vague, which left the others feeling slightly frustrated but thankfully, as he hadn't been 'turned' by Malignus; only incapacitated, he was able to remember everything else. Lucy told them about everything that had happened in the cellar from the moment Sophie had left.

Jack described what had happened to Malignus and the rest of the staff. They initially tried to see if Tom or Boz could remember anything further but quickly stopped asking, after the boys became annoyed at the constant questioning, and left them both alone.

"Tom doesn't remember anything," Sophie said with a sigh, one sunny day when they were sunbathing in one of the fields that surrounded the village. "Not even the stuff that had gone on before he was 'turned'; in fact, he barely knows who I am," she said with disappointment. "He's got James back, at least; they've been hanging out loads and that's a good thing, I suppose."

"His loss," Jack said firmly. "He's not worthy of you, Soph. You're too good for him."

She smiled at him and looked at Ben. "How's Boz doing? Have you heard much more from him?"

"Nah mate, not a thing," Ben answered, shrugging his shoulders. "He's gone a bit sulky, to be honest. Think he's a bit jealous about James and Tom being all pally again," he said, looking at Sophie. "He can still remember Tom landing James in trouble and James not speaking to them. Obviously, he can't remember how much trouble James got in, or even why James stopped speaking to them and how odd he was, but he can still remember Tom being to blame."

"What do you think is happening in school?" Sophie asked, moving the subject away from Tom. She still liked him, despite Jack's comments, and wanted to rekindle their friendship, but Tom had made it clear that he wasn't at all interested. Something she had kept to herself.

"Do we have to mention that place?" Lucy said. She was sitting in front of Jack and leaned back into him, shivering slightly. He casually wrapped his arms around her.

"Dunno," he answered, ignoring Lucy as she slapped his arms in protest for answering. "Probably trying to sort out how the fire happened and what damage was done."

"It won't come back to us, will it?" Lucy asked, panicking and tensing slightly. "We were the ones who started it."

"No it won't," Jack said, shaking his head and squeezing her gently. "Can't see how it can." He felt her relax into his arms again.

"Do you think they'll find anything else; you know, about them being monsters?" Ben asked tentatively.

"Hope so," Sophie replied.

"We'll see," Jack said. "I'd be surprised, though."

"What do you mean?" Sophie demanded.

"Well, what would they say?" he asked sarcastically. "Thornberry Woods had these big monsters, trying to get the kids and running amok throughout the school but don't worry coz they were all destroyed by a bloody big fire." He laughed out loud, "And it was a small group of plucky but pesky kids that started it all." He rolled backwards, laughing,

Lucy smacked him on the leg. "Stop messing around," she said, trying to be serious but chuckling at him.

"It'll never happen," Jack laughed, winking at them.

Sophie huffed, "Well, something should be done."

"Something was done." He smiled. "By us."

The sun shone down on where they sat. It was uncharacteristically hot and although they should have been enjoying the extra-long time away from school, and the hazy, sunny days, they couldn't quite relax properly. None of them could forget their worries about the school. Even Jack, who tried to joke and make light of it all, was concerned that something bad could happen. They all felt cold and apathetic towards anything that wasn't related to their worries, and jumped on every bit of news they could find. They were the only people who knew about the dark secret in the school and despite Jack's warnings that nothing would be said, they wanted the truth about the monsters and the Golems to be known.

47.

Lady Pravus flicked at the ash with her foot and tutted as a thin layer covered the top of her highly polished and expensive Italian stiletto shoes. The cellar was black; every inch of the ancient stone walls had been scorched in the ferocious inferno, and ash, soot and burnt debris covered everything. The explosion had destroyed half of the cellar and caused part of the passageway to collapse, meaning it had been a monumental effort to clear enough debris to allow them access. The school governors had assembled within the cellar, in an effort to explain to her what had happened. She glared at them as they waited, heads bowed in submission, for her to address them, but without saying a word she marched past them to the far end of the cellar and entered the partially collapsed space in which she knew the Sanguine had been stored. This was what she was here for; what she was interested in, not their pathetic and tiresome excuses. Her lip curled and she growled quietly to herself when she saw how badly damaged the area was. The fire brigade had eventually managed to control and extinguish the fire but the intense heat of it, combined with the highly flammable Sanguine, had caused the storage bottles to explode, destroying most of the adjacent passageway and half of the cellar, leaving glass and debris everywhere, destroying the entire crop and damaging the very foundations of the building. It would be some time before the school would be safe enough to reopen, but she was determined that it would.

Lady Pravus was old. She had held her seat at the High Council for centuries and had been instrumental in the survival of her kind. Their continued battle for existence had endured through the ages and there were forces out in the world who would do whatever it took to drive them to extinction. Her brow furrowed and she felt concern. She was one of those who had persuaded the High Council to abandon their old practices in favour of a more measured and surreptitious approach all those centuries ago and she knew how important farms such as this school were to maintaining such secrecy. Her bright blue eyes burnt with anger over the waste of such a rich harvest of Sanguine and the risk that had been presented. It had taken a lot of effort to cover up the true damage of the fire. If the existence of these farms became known to their enemies, the consequences could be immeasurable. The damage done to the school's foundations and the risks to their secrecy troubled her greatly; however, she allayed these concerns with the knowledge that no bodies had been recovered, that Veronica and her teachers had been completely obliterated, and that her counterparts who controlled such services and matters would ensure that this knowledge remained private. She returned to the main cellar and slowly but deliberately walked over to where the governors had assembled.

They stood in a small semi-circle, heads bowed in reverence, giving the respect her age and position required. Her square jaw clenched in annoyance. She was not in the mood for their pathetic simpering. "Do we yet know how this started?" she asked abruptly. "And I do not wish to hear any meandering stories."

"We believe that it may have been started deliberately, My Lady." A tall, thin man stepped forward, bowing his head low. He had a streak of white running through his otherwise jet-black hair and was clearly nervous presenting such information to his superior.

Lady Pravus's eyes narrowed. "Deliberately?"

The thin man presented a small burnt metal can. "We found this, My Lady, amidst the debris. There is no logical reason for such an item to be here." He bowed his head even lower as Lady Pravus took the scorched can of deodorant and inspected it.

She growled as she carefully looked it over. "This is human?" she whispered to herself.

The thin man cleared his throat. "We also found this, My Lady. It appeared to be hidden inside what looked to be a child's bag." He held out a small plastic bag which contained a silver crucifix and chain. Lady Pravus hissed slightly as it was presented to her. She did not touch it but looked at it with disgust. "Even more so, My Lady, we can think of no reason for this to be here other than deliberate, human involvement." He looked up as he said the last two words. His voice shook but he held Lady Pravus's gaze for a moment before looking away.

Lady Pravus turned away from the crowd of governors, letting the damaged deodorant can fall from her hand to the floor. *Could they have been compromised?* she thought warily. *Has Malignus been found out? If so, by whom? No human bones or remains were found. If indeed this was deliberate then whoever it was managed to escape the fire. Who are they? What do they know and what will they do next?*

She turned to face the governors. "You will treat this as accidental," she ordered. "Make no mention of any possible deliberate intent." She spoke forcefully and with command. She was used to her orders being followed. "It is vital that production of the Sanguine resumes as soon as possible." She took the bag holding the silver crucifix and chain from the thin man. "I will make my report of this incident to the High Council." She glared, looking him straight in the eye. "You are to ensure that repairs to the building are made, that it is made safe, and that this area is cleaned. Normal production is to be resumed as soon as possible." The thin man nodded in obedience. Lady Pravus gave him one last threatening look of contempt before marching quickly out of the cellar.

48.

*A*fter several weeks of the school being closed, letters were posted inviting pupils, parents, school partners and the wider community to attend an official school meeting, which was going to be held in the school hall one evening and would discuss all matters surrounding the fire and the next steps that the Academy would be taking. Executive members of the Triumphi in Robore Academy board would be present, as would members of the local educational authority and school governing body. There would also be opportunities for questions to be asked and answered, as well as refreshments and light snacks. Sophie, Lucy, Jack and Ben all attended the meeting with their families, whom they very quickly abandoned, preferring to sit together instead.

Seated upon the stage were members of the Academy board and the education authority, and the school governors. None of whom the four friends recognised. The strangers all looked clean-cut and smart. The men were dressed in expensive-looking black suits, whilst the women wore tailored business jackets with matching skirts. They sat upright in their chairs, prepared and watchful, looking down on the hall, alert for anything.

Jack shivered uncomfortably as he watched them whispering to each other. They made him feel uneasy and uncomfortable; they seemed to have a hidden danger.

There were three other people to the side of the stage, who looked nothing like the committee members. Mrs Harper and Mr Fields sat close to each other. She was smiling sweetly, looking over the families gathering in their seats in the hall whilst he, as usual, appeared to be dozing off. Both seemed very relaxed and comfortable in their environment. Miss Thomass was the third person. She still looked awful; if anything, worse than she had looked on the day of the fire. She appeared shaky and scared, and she sagged in her chair uncomfortably. She had large bags under her eyes and her hair looked dirty and uncombed. She looked as though she hadn't slept or washed in weeks and really didn't want to be up on the stage.

When it was time to begin, one of the Academy board members rose to his feet and stepped forward. He was a tall, skinny man and was wearing the same type of expensive sharp black suit that the other board members were wearing. His hair was jet-black, aside from a streak of white which ran through it, and he had sharp, pointy features. He cleared his throat and smiled as he addressed the hall, nodding slightly as he did. "For those of you who are unaware, my name is Mr Victor Samael and I am here to represent the Academy governing body. It is my responsibility to ensure that the school is able to swiftly recover from such a horrific and horrible incident." He gave a sombre smile as he looked across the hall. "After intensive and extensive investigation, we have been informed that a faulty gas fitting was the cause of the fire, which took hold in the school's cellar. The cellar itself was old and filled with wood and other such combustible materials, which accelerated the fire and intensified its magnitude."

Jack looked at Ben and raised an inquisitorial eyebrow. "He sounds too smug," he whispered. "And a gas main…?"

The thin man in the suit continued. "Ms Malignus and several of her staff members fought bravely and valiantly against the flames in a bid to save the school and its pupils." He bowed his head gravely, pausing for a moment. "I'm sure that by now you will be aware of the unfortunate loss of life in this most horrific tragedy. However, now that the investigation is complete, it is with deepest sympathy and regret that I am able to officially confirm that in trying to fight this vicious fire, this tragedy claimed not only Ms Malignus' life but also that of the teachers who tried to aid her." An audible gasp was heard amongst the parents in the hall. Several of them looked shocked, whilst others nodded sagely and looked mournful. Hushed conversations broke out amongst them. Mr Samael respectfully waited a moment before clearing his throat again, quietening the hall. "A memorial service will be held to respect and remember them by, details of which will be mailed to you all, and a collection will be held in aid of the local children's hospital in their honour." Again he paused, allowing his words to echo across the hall, before continuing with his announcement. "As one would expect with a fire of such voracity, extensive damage, both structural and surface, has been caused to the school. With this in mind, the Academy board and the local education authority have made the difficult decision to suspend all studies and examinations and to fully close the school whilst repairs are being carried out."

Again, chatter and conversation erupted amongst the families in the hall, each becoming slightly louder.

"We understand your concerns," he projected above the noise, "but it must be understood that during this difficult period allowances must be made to enable the school to move forward after such disaster." The hall began to settle as he continued his speech. "All children who were due to sit examinations will be awarded compensatory grades, based upon their previous academic achievement. Further details will be released shortly."

Jack looked at Lucy and shook his head in disbelief at what he was hearing. "Come on," he whispered to her, starting to get up from his seat. "I've heard enough." Quietly and discreetly, they left the hall, followed by Sophie and Ben, whilst the man in the suit continued his speech.

"What a joke!" Jack snapped as soon as they got outside and were alone.

"It's a complete cover-up," Lucy fumed, angrily shaking her head.

"I told you nothing would be done."

"It was all for nothing," Lucy said flatly. "All of it. Everything we did, everything we went through, was all for nothing."

"No," Sophie said firmly. "No, it wasn't." She looked at her friends, determined not to be defeated. "We know now, don't we? We know what's going on, and we know to look out for it. If it comes again, we'll stop it. And then we'll stop it again. And we'll keep stopping it, till it stops us."

"I wish I had your spirit," Lucy said, smiling. She reached out and hugged her friend. Sophie reciprocated, glad for the embrace.

"Sophie, I'm scared that this is just the beginning," Lucy whispered.

Just at that moment, a figure moved in the shadows.

"Who's there?" Jack snapped, turning.

All four of them followed the sound of the noise, alert and tense. A small old woman stepped into view. She was leaning on a thin walking stick and dressed all in black, with a piece of thin white material covering her head and neck. She smiled at the children.

"You're a nun?" Sophie asked. The nun bowed her head in acknowledgment.

"My name is Sister Marie O'Toole," she said, with a thick Irish accent. "And I'm afraid you are correct, child," she turned to Lucy. "This has indeed only just begun."

*T*hanks to Kath at Heddon Publishing for her expert help and advice in making this book a reality. For pulling my intelligible garble together to create this story, for always being ready with a kind word and for having the patience to answer my many trivial and often paranoid questions.

Thanks also to Loops, Sophie, Ben, Lauren, Danny, Sally, Claire and Katy (the brain trust) who helped to shape and form the narrative.

And thanks to Mona, Ethan and Neve, for never doubting, for picking me up each time I fell and for carrying me when I needed a lift. Nothing would be possible without you x

And finally, thanks to all the teachers who taught me, and those I have worked with. You have no idea how much you have contributed to this story…